BAKE IT TO THE LIMIT

Twin Berry Bakery 1

WENDY MEADOWS

Majestic Owl Publishing LLC
P.O. Box 997
Newport, NH 03773

1

Rita Knight glared at her twin sister with her usual aggravated expression. “Why?” she asked.

“Because,” Rhonda Knight responded in a humorous voice as she slapped a smiley face sticker onto the side of an old-fashioned cash register that now belonged to the Twin Berry Bakery. “A smiley face a day keeps the doctor away...or doctors, in our case, because we're both forty-four and not spring chickens anymore.”

Rita glanced down at the soft green dress she hoped made her appear distinguished yet youthful. The dress was very lovely—and costly—and complimented her flowy strawberry blonde hair, but her sister’s words suddenly made her feel more like a simple green bean stuck in a rusted can. “Don't remind me of our age,” she begged Rhonda. “Yesterday had to be the worst birthday we have ever experienced.”

Rhonda grinned. “Humor makes life better, sister.”

Rita rolled her eyes. She loved her sister more than life but could never understand why the woman had the heart of a clown. “Logic is strength,” she fired back, holding firm to her lifelong belief in the value of taking life seriously. Comedy was one of many frivolous distractions to be discarded along with other nonsense that interrupted practical life.

“Oh, pooh,” Rhonda replied and motioned her hands around at the lovely bakery that looked like a kitchen straight out of the nineteen-thirties. “Just look at our new bakery,” she said and then added with a happy smile: “The bank wouldn't have given us the loan if I hadn't made the loan officer laugh at my jokes.”

“It was my business plan that did the trick. And that dress you’re wearing is a joke,” Rita complained, cringing at the sight of the bright yellow and pink dress her sister was wearing. “You look like a deranged pink lemonade.”

Rhonda threw her hand at Rita. “Oh, you wouldn't smile even if you won the lottery,” she said.

Rita rolled her eyes. “Winning the lottery isn't practical. Owning and managing a business that can support daily, monthly, and yearly expenses is practical. Need I remind you we have a mortgage, two car payments, and other financial obligations that need our attention?” Rita nervously glanced around the deserted bakery and wondered if going into business with her sister had been practical. The bakery was lovely and the building itself held a certain appeal. The old hardwood floor was very nice and the vintage wood-paneled walls did make a person feel as if they had stepped back in time. The only items that needed to be replaced were a few splintery old wooden shelves and a cracked glass display case sitting to the side of the front counter. "A little fresh paint...some flowers...but what it needs is a touch of class on the walls. We could update this whole place—"

"Hold it," Rhonda objected, reading her sister like a book, "I know what you're thinking and the answer is no."

"No?" Rita prepared for an argument. "Rhonda, if we're going to be successful we—"

"We're not going to transform this lovely bakery into a cookie-cutter modern art gallery," Rhonda told Rita in a stern voice. "In today's world all you see are look-a-likes...everywhere. Towns all look the same, buildings, grocery stores...why, I can't tell one town apart from the next anymore. Chain stores are everywhere...corporate America has ruined the character of our great land—"

"Oh, please don't give me one of your speeches about how corporations are destroying America," Rita begged. "I hear enough of your crazy conspiracy theories at home."

Rhonda folded her arms and gave Rita one of her I-Feel-Sorry-For-You looks. "If you would only open your eyes," she said in a desperate voice. "But...okay, I'll bypass my speech and just say this bakery will take a hard nose dive if we transform it into a flashy modern dump just like all the others that pollute the American landscape. We need originality...we need to reach back into time and bring the good old days back alive. We need to give this bakery a heart."

Rita hated to agree with her sister on any topic, but the vintage appeal of the building was undeniable and she had to admit that making the bakery into a modern look-a-like wasn't very practical. "Rhonda, the loan officer approved our business loan because our credit was stable and because we're both retired cops with savings and small pensions to fall back on. But if this bakery fails, we're both going to be dipping into our personal savings to pay back the business loan...for a long time. Now, with that said, I don't want to argue. I simply want to agree that making this bakery a success will become our primary...and only...goal. And with that said...I do agree that a vintage design would be....helpful to our goal of owning a successful business."

"You bet," Rhonda said and tapped the smiley face sticker on the side of the old cash register and beamed with excitement. "I knew this would work out when we left Atlanta. Moving to this lovely small town up here in North Georgia was the best idea we ever had...not to mention buying ourselves our (a) lovely two-story cabin on a piece of land with a river running through it...oh, this life is the fulfillment of my dream."

"I thought your dream was to live in Los Angeles and become a star?" Rita asked, teasing her sister.

"Oh well...you know...being a cop got in the way," Rhonda blushed.

Rita rolled her eyes. “Sure it did,” she told Rhonda. “My, how time flies. Doesn’t it seem like just yesterday we went through the police academy after we left the Navy? So let's see, if we enlisted in the Navy right when we turned eighteen, completed our contract...and then we went to the academy one year later...that would make it--”

“Twenty years ago,” Rhonda sighed. “Twenty long years ago.”

Rita saw joy leave her sister's face. “Oh, I'm sorry, Rhonda. I was only trying to tease you.”

“I know,” Rhonda sighed again. “It's just that...well, it’s not the silly dream of being a movie star I think about. I think about love and making a family. I’m still not married and neither are you, Rita. And being single at forty-four is no laughing matter. I can laugh at almost anything...except being unmarried.” Rhonda reached into a green purse sitting on the front counter and pulled out a half-eaten bran muffin wrapped in a soft pink handkerchief. “See this?”

“Your breakfast?”

“My predictable, lousy breakfast,” Rhonda pointed out. “I bypass the junk food, walk five miles a day, take my daily vitamins, sleep eight hours a night...everything I’ve been doing since high school, because deep down I believe someday I'll find Mr. Right and actually get married.” Rhonda looked down at the bran muffin, made a sour face, and tossed it down onto the counter. “It’s stupid. I don’t know why I bother.”

Rita studied her sister’s upset face. “I know you're upset,” she said in a loving voice, stepping away from business for a minute and becoming a caring sister again, "but until love peeks its beautiful eyes around the corner, I'm afraid we have no other choice but to keep living our lives and doing what makes us happy. And doesn't this bakery make us happy?"

Rhonda looked away from Rita and tossed her eyes at the glass front. "Yes, I suppose you're right." Fall leaves were dancing in the crisp, early morning autumn air gently caressing the small town of Clovedale Falls. The sight of the autumn leaves created a cozy, warm feeling in her heart that slowly pushed away the sadness trying to destroy the peaceful morning. "Maybe I'll find a husband at the Pumpkin Festival?" she said in a hopeful voice.

Rita sighed. Being a twin sister meant she felt every single ounce of pain Rhonda felt—and more, at times; even though she would never admit the truth of this. Rita understood Rhonda's painful longing to fall in love, get married, and begin a family. She too longed to wake up to a husband and share a cup of coffee with him and raise babies and spend rainy nights playing board games with children. But there was no way to hurry fate along. "The Pumpkin Festival starts in a few days", she said in a loving voice.

"A few days," Rhonda replied and quickly forced a smile back to her face. There was no sense in letting a foolish heart ruin a beautiful day. "You know, Rita," she said, "we bought a beautiful cabin together. And now we're opening our own bakery. And you're right. So what if Mr. Right hasn't come along yet? When he does...if he does...great. Until then, well, life goes on and so do we. Now," as she grabbed her bran muffin and tossed it into a wooden trash can under the front counter, "let's focus on the here and now."

Rita felt a calm smile touch her face. Her sister was a fighter and never let life push her down for too long. That was one character trait about Rhonda that Rita admired more than anything: Rhonda never gave up and always went all twelve rounds even when the fight seems lost. Rita on the other hand had a bad tendency to give up the fight when logic screamed in her ears it was futile, instead of letting faith carry her through to the conclusion. "Back to business. I agree that we need not design our bakery in a modern scheme," she said. "I believe an old fashioned design will be fun and profitable."

"Which means we have a whole lot of antique stores to visit," Rhonda pointed out excitedly. "Clovedale Falls has a few antique stores and I believe I saw a couple in Dove Hills, and--"

"Wait a minute," Rita objected and quickly held up her right hand. "Rhonda, we're not rich. We can't spend all our savings in antique stores. We have to be practical."

"We also have to spend money to make money," Rhonda pointed out. "Atmosphere is everything, Rita." Rhonda pointed to the front window. "We can bake the best muffins and cakes in town but if we don't set the right atmosphere...splat!" Rhonda smashed her hands together. "Like a bug hitting a windshield."

“I really don't think--”

“We'll get off to a good start and then...splat!” Rhonda smashed her hands together again. “Like a bug with no sense buzzing down a night highway.”

Rita stared at her sister. Fear quickly gripped her heart. “Rhonda, this is our first time ever owning a business. We spent so many years fighting crime. Relocating to Clovedale Falls...going into business for ourselves...buying the cabin...this is all so very risky and scary. I simply want to make sure that we don't fail and by chance, if we do, we have a little money to fall back on. I'm wary about spending more money than we have allocated for our start-up funds.”

Rhonda understood Rita's worry. Deep down she was scared herself. “I promise we'll stick within our budget,” she told Rita and offered a warm smile. “This bakery isn't the size of an iceberg. It won't take a lot to make this place look like the nineteen-thirties. A few tables, some shelves, and we'll be off and running.”

“Off and running,” Rita said in a nervous voice. “That means we must bake...and that's where the true test will come.” Rita gazed around the bakery. “That is, if we even get past the health inspector.”

Rhonda bit down on her lip. “Yeah...the health inspector,” she agreed and looked at the wooden door leading back into the kitchen. “The kitchen is a mess, isn't it?”

“We need all new appliances--”

“Which is covered by our loan,” Rhonda pointed out.

“I know,” Rita said in a grateful voice. “I can't imagine what we would have paid out of pocket for the new appliances we need to get the kitchen back in functioning order.”

Rhonda was more worried about the health inspector. She didn't believe the jokes she told the loan officer would go over well with the health inspector, who was a sixty-nine-year-old woman named Mrs. Thorndale. Rumor was—at least from the mouth of the loan officer—Mrs. Thorndale was meaner than a threatened rattlesnake and colder than a block of ice dredged up from an underground ice cave. According to the loan officer, Mrs. Thorndale was tougher than a Marine drill sergeant with inspections and searched for any excuse to fail a hopeful business owner. Rhonda tried to banish those thoughts from her mind. “I know we can do it. We have one week before the health inspector is due to arrive. That's plenty of time to get our bakery in tip-top shape. We have money in our loan to cover the new appliances and we have a few extra dollars set aside for buying what we need to transform this front room into something that reminds folks of the old days. As long we keep a positive attitude, I think we'll succeed in all our efforts.”

“Prayer first,” Rita pointed out in a serious voice.

“Yes, prayer,” Rhonda agreed. She grimaced and tried to turn it into a smile. “With our baking--”

“Our baking skills are--”

"Decent," Rhonda finished for Rita and forced a worried smile to her face. "We may never bake the best coconut cake in the world, sister, but we don't burn our cookies in the oven. This a small town and folks here are used to granny's cookies...we have a lot of competition to overcome in order to make a go of it."

"You're not making me feel very confident," Rita complained, looking around at the dusty corners of the room behind her.

Rhonda winced. "I guess I'm just as nervous as you are," she admitted. "I know I haven't been showing it, but I'm...well, I'm nervous, okay? We have invested our lives into this bakery and our new home. If we fail...you and I both know our personal savings won't quite cut it. It will be Mom and Dad bailing us out of a deep hole."

"Then let's not fail," Rita begged.

"Yeah, let's not," Rhonda agreed, "because I don't want to ask Mom and Dad for help. They were so happy when we retired from the force and moved to Clovedale Falls--" Rhonda stopped talking when the front door opened and a woman in her mid-sixties strolled inside just as relaxed as a soft autumn breeze. "Oh, I'm terribly sorry, we're not open for business yet," Rhonda said in a quick voice.

Erma Wilson tossed a warm smile at Rhonda and then smiled at Rita. "I know you're not open for business," she said in a honeyed voice filled with gentle love that nearly melted Rita and Rhonda down to the floor. "I've just come to see my old bakery."

"Your bakery?" Rita asked in pleased surprise as her eyes absorbed the woman's short gray hair and round, rosy face that cried grandmotherly and now, most important, delicious baker.

The woman smiled at Rita, folded her wrinkled, arthritic hands in front of her soft, rust-colored dress patterned with leaves, and nodded. "My name is Mrs. Erma Wilson and I owned this bakery for forty years," she explained. "Five years ago...after my Ralph went on to Heaven and my hands became too stiff and poorly to bake anymore...I closed up shop and put the building up for sale." Erma's sweet smile slowly faded. "I'm afraid the building has sat empty these last five years, collecting dust. And last year, a couple of runts broke in here and made a mess of things. Sheriff Bluestone put them to work mowing a whole lot of the town."

Rita and Rhonda looked at each other in surprise and then focused back on Erma. "Uh...we are pleased to meet you, Mrs. Wilson. Can I offer you some coffee?" Rita asked. "We brought some in a thermos."

"Oh no," Erma replied and brought her smile back like a ray of sunshine. "I just came back to meet the two women who bought my bakery and to thank you. Ralph didn't leave me much to live on and now, with your purchase, I have enough money to rest on. Thanks to you--" Tears began to sting at (in) the elderly woman's eyes. "Oh my dears, excuse me," she said and hurried back outside, leaving Rita and Rhonda confused.

"One of us should go outside and comfort her," Rita said, staring at Erma through the front window. Erma stood outside on the front sidewalk wiping at her eyes with a white handkerchief embroidered with little autumn pumpkins.

"Be my guest," Rhonda offered. "I've never been good with…the gooey stuff. I always played the bad cop when we interrogated crooks, remember?"

"Except you were horrible at playing bad cop," Rita reminded her sister.

"Don't remind me," Rhonda complained.

"You could never keep a straight face," Rita said and shook her head.

"I know, I know," Rhonda replied. "I would always get tickled at myself."

"That's because you wouldn't stop looking at your face in the two-way mirror!"

Rhonda blushed. "I always thought in the interrogation room...it felt like acting, and I wanted to see what I might have looked like if I were an actress on the big screen…" Rhonda shook her head. "Oh, forget it. I know I was no good at it. Just please go comfort her, Rita."

Rita looked up and then quickly dropped her gazed back down at her hands. "No need…she is coming back inside," she said quietly.

Rhonda dropped her eyes and studied the floor, hoping Erma hadn't noticed that she and Rita had been staring at her.

"Please forgive me for rushing out in such a way," Erma said in a sweet voice. "I'm a very sentimental person and when I step inside my bakery...my heart releases years and years of cherished memories."

"Oh, that's...okay," Rhonda assured Erma in a polite voice, patting the woman on the arm awkwardly. She looked at Erma's soft face, and her grandmotherly countenance was not only soothing, but reassuring. It was like the woman's presence somehow calmed all of their worries and fears in just one round. "The loan officer didn't tell us who owned the bakery," she said to change the subject.

"Willy Matthews doesn't care for my bakery," Erma pointed out. "Mr. Mathews has had it out for me ever since I refused to marry him decades ago. I was beginning to fear that old skunk would never sell my bakery." Erma set down her brown crocodile skin pocketbook on the dusty front counter. "There have been interested buyers before you two women came along. But for whatever reason, Willy Matthews would never approve a loan."

Rita looked at Rhonda. Rhonda shrugged her eyebrows. "Well, we're very happy our loan was approved, Mrs. Wilson," Rita said.

Erma lovingly looked around the bakery. “My Ralph's daddy owned this building for many years and gave it to us as a wedding present. Ralph wanted to start a hardware store but I begged him to let me start my very own bakery. Ralph was so sweet and agreed.”

Rhonda felt the nervous ball in her stomach uncoil and disappear as she pictured Erma and Ralph setting up their bakery so many decades ago. “That's so sweet,” she said.

“Well, he might have been swayed for a couple reasons,” Erma teased, “because Ralph knew I baked the best cake in all of Georgia. He figured if he let me start my own bakery he would be getting all the free cake he wanted.”

Rita felt a smile touch her lips. There was something very special about Erma, something she couldn't put her finger on. “I'm sure he came out the winner.”

“We both did,” Erma assured Rita. “When my Ralph passed away...he left a big empty hole inside of me.” Tears stung her eyes again. Mrs. Wilson drew in a deep breath and steadied herself. “My Ralph was on a hunting trip way up in Montana. A few of his old buddies brought their grandkids along...Ralph and I never could have children.” Erma paused, looked around the bakery again, and continued. “One of the kids accidentally shot my Ralph.”

“Oh, that's horrible,” Rhonda exclaimed. Rita’s hands flew up to cover her mouth in shock.

“Yes, it was,” Erma agreed. “But the Good Lord has His reasons and I'm not to question them. I had forty good years with my Ralph and all of Heaven waiting. In the meantime I know my Ralph is looking down on me with a big smile on his face." Erma looked at Rhonda and then over to Rita. "When I closed my bakery I took all of my furnishings and kitchen things away. I was very upset and sadly, bitter. But time has healed my pain." Erma forced her sweet smile back to her face. "I have no use for all those things now. If you would like, perhaps...you two would like my old belongings and bring them back where they belong, bring them back home to the bakery?" she asked in a hopeful voice.

"Really?" Rhonda asked in an awed voice. Rita squeezed her sister's hand, not wanting her sister to appear too forward at the woman's generous offer, yet knowing it was just the help they needed.

Erma nodded. "I have furnishings in storage and an attic full of boxes holding years of memories that belong in this bakery." Erma looked at Rhonda and Rita. "Please don't get upset with me for saying this...but I always worried whoever bought my bakery would...take away the heart of my bakery and replace it with something ugly—something that just didn't keep to the feel of the old fashioned way I used to run things. It would mean so much if you two ladies would...remember the old days." Erma looked down at her arthritic hands. "Of course, you can design the bakery any which way you see fit ... it is your bakery now. The papers are signed and ownership has been transferred over to you."

"Erma," Rhonda promised in a soft voice, "before you arrived, my sister and I were just discussing how to decorate the bakery. We agreed on an old nineteen-thirties look. It just fits perfectly with this place, we can feel it. We feel a modern look would ruin any chance we might have at succeeding."

"That's right," Rita chimed in. "Rhonda and I even have money set aside to visit antique shops and search out relics...err, items...that would fit the atmosphere we're after."

Erma raised her head. Absolute happiness filled her eyes. "Oh, the touch of time you need is simply waiting for you in my attic," she promised in an overjoyed voice.

Rhonda smiled. "I bet it is," she told Erma. "Say, we better introduce ourselves before we go any further. My name is Rhonda Knight and this is my sister Rita Knight."

"Hello," Rita smiled at Erma.

Erma smiled back. "Rita and Rhonda Knight. You're the retired cops from Atlanta. Not yet married, no children." Erma winked at Rita. "In Clovedale Falls, news travels fast."

"I guess it does," Rhonda said in a stunned voice. "I thought my sister and I had been keeping a low profile."

Erma smiled again. "Keeping a low profile at the old Hardcastle cabin on the little river?" she added.

"Wow, news does travel fast," Rhonda gasped.

"Folks like to know who their new neighbors are," Erma explained. "You bought Mr. Hardcastle's old cabin. That cabin sits on a very nice piece of land...one of the prettiest places in the county, if you ask me. But Mr. Hardcastle was a hard man who wouldn't sell to just anyone. When he sold his cabin and left town folks became mighty curious."

Rita gave her sister a confused look. "Erma, we only met Mr. Hardcastle a handful of times."

"Once when we toured the cabin," Rhonda explained.

"A second time when we asked to see the cabin again before we drew up our offer," Rita added.

"And a third time on the day we signed the papers and closed the sale," Rhonda finished.

Erma shrugged her shoulders. "All I know is there was a lot of folk wanting that cabin and you two were the ones Mr. Hardcastle sold to. Seems to me," Erma smiled, "you two were meant to become part of Clovedale Falls."

Rita and Rhonda looked at each other and then focused back on Erma. "I guess maybe we were?" Rhonda told Erma, feeling a strange but wonderful feeling course through her heart. "Uh...maybe if you'd like, you can help us...decorate the bakery?" she asked and looked at Rita for confirmation.

Rita nodded. "That would be very nice," she agreed. "If you owned and operated this bakery for forty years then I know you're a woman who understands how to make a business become a success."

"The only way you will walk in my shoes without falling down is by keeping the heart of this bakery alive," Erma explained in a heartfelt voice that sent chills of excitement down Rita and Rhonda's spines. "The heart is what matters and the heart will bring customers through that front door, customers that will become like family to you. If you treat this bakery like a business and treat people like walking money signs, you'll fall flat on your faces and be turned away into the wind."

Rhonda drew in a deep breath. "Erma, you have a lot to teach us," she said.

"Yes, a lot," Rita agreed and then added: "What a blessing it was that you visited us this morning."

"You two are the blessing," Erma told Rita. "I was very afraid I would encounter two no-nonsense women offended at my nosiness, simply reject my offer and run me out onto the street." Erma looked around the bakery again and sighed. "People today are always wanting to change things for no reason, and usually for the worse...they're never satisfied with the way things are. My daddy worked at a sawmill his entire life. My momma worked sewing dresses. We weren't rich or poor. The good Lord provided food on the table and a roof over our head. And you know what?"

"What?" Rita asked.

"Life was good...precious," Erma said in a voice that slowly drifted off into memories tinged with sadness. "The old days were the good days. But the old days are being forgotten...being replaced by something I don't even recognize anymore. I hardly ever leave Clovedale Falls, but when I do, I don't recognize the world I see. I just stay at my old house on Maple Frost Lane, tend to my garden and flower beds. I come into town and do my grocery shopping, visit with some friends, and go home. And that's the way I like it. The simple life."

Rhonda stared at Erma for a few seconds. The sadness glowing in Erma's eyes reached out and touched her heart. "I think that's the kind of life that drew us here to with this small community. I hope maybe...what I mean to say is...we would like to become your friends."

"Yes, we would," Rita said in a quick voice, shocked at her sudden words. She was a woman who thought matters through and never rushed into a decision, yet she felt the need to secure a special friendship with Erma. Why? Rita didn't know.

"I would like that," Erma promised. "I would like that much. And maybe...if you'd like, I can come by every now and then and help out in the bakery? I would love it."

"Especially with the Pumpkin Festival coming up…we'd like to use it to launch our bakery so everyone can get to know us. We would love your help," Rita assured Erma.

"And we would treasure your company," Rhonda added.

Erma smiled and spoke but was interrupted when the front door burst open and a very scared elderly woman came bustling inside. "Call the sheriff," the woman yelled in a terrified voice. "Somebody call the sheriff."

Erma steadied the woman by her shoulders. “Lilly DeLoach, calm yourself a second. What in the world?” she gasped.

Lilly stared at Erma with wide, terrified eyes. Rita and Rhonda recognized her as the woman in her early seventies who owned a cozy candle shop next door to the bakery—she ran it with the help of a few younger helpers and was not usually alone in her shop. The couple times they had run into her, the sisters had come away knowing her as someone funny, charming, and full of vigor, not the type of woman to scare easily. She was a product of the old days who kept throwing punches. “A dead...a dead body,” she told Erma through great gasps of air, “right there in the front room...”

Erma hugged Lilly tightly and tried to calm her.

“A dead body?” Rhonda asked, almost in shock but feeling the familiar patterns of cop work steady her nerves. She glanced calmly at Rita. “We better go take a look.”

Rita nodded. “Get your gun out of your purse.”

“Oh dear,” Erma said, holding her friends and watching Rita and Rhonda transform into cops. “A dead body? Lilly, are you sure?”

“A man...lying face-down on the hardwood floor,” Lilly nodded and buried her head in Erma’s shoulder.

Rita and Rhonda quickly retrieved two Glock 19s and hurried to the front door. "Erma, call the sheriff," Rita ordered. "Rhonda and I will have a look."

"Right next door in my candle shop," Lilly explained.

"We've been in your candle shop," Rhonda told Lilly. "We know our way." And with those words, Rhonda stepped outside in the wind with her gun lowered down to her side. "Let's not spook anyone," she told Rita.

Rita looked up and down the front street, spotted nothing amiss down the row of cozy gingerbread buildings holding different shops, and then looked up at the crisp, blue sky. The morning was beautiful—so beautiful—and blessedly empty. Not a person was in sight. "Let's hurry," she told Rhonda.

Rhonda nodded and made her way toward the front door of Lilly's candle shop. Lilly sold every kind of peppermint candle a person could imagine, along with holiday-themed candles shaped like cozy snow villages. The candles were hand designed by a local man who remained anonymous but whose work brought in buyers from all over the world. "Ready?"

"Ready," Rita nodded.

Rhonda drew in a deep breath, pulled open a wooden door decorated around the window frame with peppermint stripes, and entered into a shop that smelled of peppermint and chocolate. The front room held rows and rows of low wooden shelves full of candles, but what stood out the most was the large wooden table in the room. The table, draped with a snow-white cloth, displayed a large snowy Christmas village made of only candles. But Rhonda didn't have time to admire the snowy village. Her eyes went straight to a dead man lying face down on the polished hardwood floor. “We have a body,” she told Rita in a miserable voice.

“I'll cover you,” Rita said, looking around the front room. “You check the body.”

Rhonda hurried over to the body, knowing that her sister always had a weak stomach, knelt down, and examined the body. “Body is cold,” she called out. “Checking for identification and--”

“And what?” Rita asked.

Rhonda quickly stood up and backed away from the body. “Hey, this isn't our job anymore,” she pointed out. “We're not cops anymore, remember? We're retired.”

Rita looked at her sister and then slowly and regretfully nodded. “You're right,” she said. “Old habits die hard.”

“Yes, they do,” Rhonda explained. She looked at the body. As she did her eyes became curious. “You know, if I knew no better I'd say I know that guy.”

Rita locked her eyes on him. She saw a man in his late fifties with dark gray hair. The man was wearing an outdated, cheap gray suit that sat snug around his belly. “He does look familiar, doesn't he?” she asked.

“Yes, he does,” Rhonda said and dared to approach the body again. She knelt down, put her eyes all the way down on the floor, and got a glimpse of the man’s face. “Oh my!” she exclaimed.

“What?” Rita demanded.

“We do know this guy,” Rhonda called out. “Rita, this is Joey 'The Bookie' Stally.”

Rita froze. “Joey...but he's in the Witness Protection Program.”

“Not anymore,” Rhonda said and stood up.“If Joey is here and he's dead, that means…”

“Don't say it,” Rita said in a scared voice and glanced nervously around the small confines of the shop, “because I know what you're thinking.”

2

Sheriff Brad Bluestone, better known as Sheriff Rawhide because of his cattle ranching family, watched the shiny black hearse pull away from the candle shop and ease down Main Street like a creepy finger pointing the way to a cold secret. "Doc Downing said the man was poisoned," he told Rita and Rhonda in a voice toughened and hard.

Rita looked at the sheriff with worried eyes and studied his leathery face worn by years of ranching in the hot sun and serving as sheriff over the sprawling hills of the county. The man was well into his late fifties but looked tougher than a rattlesnake preparing to do battle with a mountain lion. His eyes were hooded deep below his protruding, dark brows—eyes that reminded Rita of a lone cowboy lost in a futuristic world. He held his hat in one hand, watching the hearse turn off Main Street and disappear around a corner, and the wind ruffled through his thin gray hair.

Rita felt concerned for how this no-nonsense lawman would respond to her and her sister interfering with his crime scene, and had prepared a long, serious explanation for their motives. “Sheriff, let me first explain--”

Brad held up his right hand as a strong breeze brushed against his military pressed gray and brown uniform. “Mrs. Knight, you and your sister didn't do no harm. A cop doesn't stop being a cop just because a piece of paper says they retired.”

Rhonda stepped up next to Rita. Her nerves were tight and her heart was filled with a deep worry that clung with cruel fingers. She wanted to confess to the sheriff that Joey 'The Bookie' Stally was someone she and her sister both knew, but didn't, not yet. She didn’t know whether to reveal his past from before the Witness Protection Program, and so erred on the side of caution. Besides, Brad Bluestone was still a stranger and, no strangers could be trusted, not even the local sheriff. “We appreciate that, Sheriff,” she said in an even voice that clearly hid her worry. “My sister and I simply reacted. I guess old instincts die hard.”

Rita looked at Rhonda, read her sister’s eyes, and understood. “I hate to ask this at a sensitive time, but it effects our business, too…will you cancel the Pumpkin Festival?” she asked.

Brad shook his head no. “That festival brings a lot of money into this town,” he explained. “Folks from all over come this time of year. If I cancel the festival all the local business owners will suffer and get real mad at me in return.” Brad looked up and down the main street.

"Clovedale Falls is a quiet little town. A town where folks are born and raised or retire to when they get old. Towns like this need tourists to survive. The Pumpkin Festival brings in enough revenue to help folks get by in the lean months. I know you ladies understand."

Rita looked toward the bakery. She understood all right. "We understand," she assured Brad. "Our bakery opens in one week."

"Festival runs for two months," Brad explained. "October through November." Brad studied the quiet street. "Town is quiet right now. Folks don't start piling in until the middle of October. The old folks, those who don't handle crowds too good, come in early October and fill up the first two weeks. The last two weeks of October are crammed with folks...elbow to elbow. The first couple of weeks of November stay full but the last two weeks thin out and let the late-comers enjoy the remainder of the festival without having to search for a parking space. The weather is cooler by then but folks seem to like it that way. It's a lot of logistics to manage but we've got it down to something of a science."

Rhonda listened to Brad explain the plans for traffic management during the event. The man's words somehow seemed to deflate the magic, cozy feeling that came to life in her about Erma's help and the upcoming festival. Sure, she understood the town's side of the festival and the need to keep people safe, parking open, traffic moving, and business going. But in her heart she only wanted to see a warm and cozy place filled with hot apple fritters, apple cider drinks, hayrides, pumpkin patch visits, and other wonderful treasures that filled the heart with happiness that only the sight of colorful leaves falling in crisp afternoon air could explain. Hearing Brad talking about the flip side of the festival was depressing—and Rhonda didn't like being depressed. Humor was her usual defense against the world. Yet she didn't feel like digging up a joke just now. A man was dead—a man connected to the mafia. "We'll be open for the crowds," she assured Brad in an attempt to return back to the warm side of the Pumpkin Festival.

Brad looked at their bakery. "I moved here about twenty years ago," he explained, "after spending twenty years as a cop out in Phoenix. I guess I was a little older than you two ladies are now." Brad placed his hands behind his back. "I grew tired of the violence, the crime, the corruption...couldn't stand it anymore. Got to the point where I dreaded putting on my badge. When I retired, my wife and I moved here."

"Why Clovedale Falls?" Rita asked.

"The Pumpkin Festival, for one," Brad explained. "My wife is from this area and every year, like clockwork, we would come for two weeks." Brad kept his eyes on the bakery as if he was searching for an old memory. "About a year before I retired from the force my son went into the Navy. Didn't see no sense in staying in Phoenix. My wife and me talked it over and moved here."

"How did you end up as the sheriff?" Rhonda asked.

"You know how these things go," Brad replied. "We took over my wife's family's ranching business but it was never enough to keep me busy. And then about a year after we settled down, Sheriff Callum retired. A deputy sheriff named Jeff Mayes took over for a while but was forced to quit when the Georgia Bureau of Investigations investigated him. Never found out for what...didn't ask." Brad finally took his eyes away from the bakery and looked at Rita and Rhonda. "Jeff Mayes hit the road only a couple of weeks before the Pumpkin Festival was about to start. The city council was in a panic."

"I bet," Rita said.

Brad nodded. "Clovedale Falls usually employs one sheriff and three deputies. During the Pumpkin Festival, additional deputies are hired on...local people looking to make extra money. Folks you put in charge of directing traffic and telling people where to park." Brad glanced up at the sky and then back at Rita and Rhonda. "Wasn't long before the city council came knocking at my door and offering me a temporary job as sheriff. Their younger deputies on the force weren't quite experienced enough at the time to take on the head job. I refused at first, but my wife pressured me into accepting the job. Anyways, when the festival ended, I stayed on to help out and when elections came around folks made it official."

"Why did you stay on?" Rita asked.

"Same reason you ladies ran into the candle shop," Brad told Rita. "You don't stop being a cop because a piece of paper says you retired. I tried to stop being a cop but the cop life wouldn't leave me alone." Brad glanced around with a grin crinkling the corners of his eyes, but then the fondness faded from his face as he turned back to them. "Clovedale Falls isn't Phoenix. This town is filled with families and old folks like myself. Up until this morning about the only trouble we ever had was a few speeders."

Rhonda felt guilt strike her heart. She looked at Rita and saw the same guilt strike her sister. They had brought trouble into a cozy, warm, safe community filled with sweet families and gentle old folks who spent their days making candles, carving wood, and baking cakes. "I..." she began to say but then stopped. The sheriff was a stranger and Joey 'The Bookie' Stally was a man the mafia wanted dead...and most likely found and killed him. If she confessed the truth to Brad, well, the sheriff himself—if put under pressure—might spill the beans. Caution had to be used. Since Joey was dead, that meant the mafia might come after anyone else involved in that long-ago case. Perhaps even two retired cops who had just opened a bakery.

"What?" Brad asked, seeing the hesitation on her face.

"I need to get back to the bakery," Rhonda said in a quick voice. "Erma is waiting."

"Yes," Rita supported Rhonda's words, "we need to get back. We have a great deal of work to do before the health inspector arrives and we can open."

Brad removed his hands from behind his back, reached into his front right pocket, brought out an old wooden pipe, and nodded his head. "I'm guessing Erma will help you ladies out a little," he said.

"Erma has offered to help us," Rita confirmed as Brad fiddled for an old lighter and finally lit his pipe. The sweet smell of cherry tobacco streamed out into the air in snowy white puffs of fragrant smoke that complemented the late morning.

"If you wouldn't mind," Rhonda said in a quick voice, "will you keep us informed?"

"Not sure how a dead man ended up in Lilly's candle shop," Brad said, puffing on his pipe. "Not ready to ask the state for any help, either. I'll talk to Lilly, ask a few questions, and see what I can dig up."

Rita glanced at Rhonda and then back at Brad. "Are you familiar with homicide cases?" she asked.

Brad nodded his head. "Worked homicide before I retired," he explained. "It's been brought to my attention you two ladies worked homicide yourselves down in Atlanta."

"That part of our lives is over with," Rita assured Brad even though the deepest part of her heart knew that was more of a hopeful statement than a real truth.

"I doubt it," Brad replied. "Once a cop always a cop...at least for the good apples in the barrel. You two don't seem like bad apples."

"All we want to do is settle down, live a nice, quiet life, and run our bakery," Rhonda told Brad. "We retired and left Atlanta because, like you, we grew tired of the violence and crime...grew tired of the ugliness people did to one another. We want to...rest our hearts, Sheriff. I hope you can understand that."

"I understand," Brad told Rhonda and nodded toward the bakery. "Send Lilly out to me, okay?"

"Will do," Rhonda promised and hurried Rita away.

"Ladies?" Brad called out just as Rhonda opened the front door to the bakery.

"Yes?" Rhonda called out over her shoulder, turning.

"When you're ready, you can tell me why you're keeping the truth from me," Brad said and puffed on his pipe again, looking out at the street unperturbed.

Rhonda and Rita stared at Brad. The sheriff was more intelligent than he looked. "Rita?" Rhonda asked in a low, urgent tone.

"Not yet," Rita whispered and hurried her sister back inside the bakery. "Uh, Lilly, Sheriff Bluestone wants to speak with you," she told a nervous, scared old woman.

Lilly DeLoach squeezed Erma's hand. "I'll call you," she promised and nervously made her way outside.

Erma waited until the front door closed before she spoke. "Is Sheriff Rawhide going to cancel the Pumpkin Festival?" she asked in a worried voice.

"No," Rita told Erma, glancing over her shoulder at Rhonda. Her eyes said what they both knew to be true: they had to get the bakery operational. They didn't have time to deal with a murder.

"Sheriff Rawhide—er, Sheriff Bluestone explained to us how the Pumpkin Festival keeps Clovedale Falls alive," Rhonda explained. "We didn't realize just how important the festival is until today."

Erma walked over to Rita and Rhonda. "Your neighbors will keep your heads above water in bad times," she said in a serious voice, "but the tourist trade will save you from going under. Without the Pumpkin Festival, Clovedale Falls would die." Erma looked at the front door. "A dead man in town...my, when word gets out..."

Rita and Rhonda exchanged worried glances. They both understood that if the Pumpkin Festival failed, they would fail. The sudden realization sobered their minds about the true reality of the business world: people had to be happy enough and safe enough to spend money on what you were selling. If the tourists became scared or spooked by the crime, then that meant no money. Of course, money wasn't the only objective—the joy of owning a business was a reward in itself, yet, money was needed to survive. "We have to focus on the bakery," Rita said.

"We have one week before the health inspector arrives," Rhonda agreed.

"But we can't ignore the truth," Rita pointed out, not stating the obvious but signaling to her sister that they had urgent business to discuss.

"No, we can't," Rhonda agreed.

"Your thoughts?" Rita asked.

"I'm not sure," Rhonda replied. She looked around and spoke to Erma. "Erma, my sister and I need to be alone," she said in a polite voice. "We need to talk about our plans."

"I understand," Erma promised, not offended. "I should go check on Lilly anyway." She picked up her pocketbook and eased over to the front door. "Supper will be ready at six sharp. I'm making my homemade squash soup with cornbread and pound cake for dessert. Don't be late."

"But--" Rita began to object.

"But nothing," Erma said in a stern but loving voice and then tossed her address over her shoulder as she left. "Don't be late," she said and left the bakery before Rita or Rhonda could get a word out.

Rhonda looked down at her hands. After Brad had arrived, she and Rita had put their guns back in the bakery. Standing empty-handed made her feel scared and vulnerable. "It's not supposed to be like this," she told Rita, feeling anger flush in her cheeks. "We moved to Clovedale Falls to get away from the ugliness. How did Joey The Bookie end up dead next door to us?"

Rita fully felt her sister's fear and anger and searched her mind. “If the DeVivo Family is in Clovedale Falls, we're in trouble,” she pointed out. “Joey was in the Witness Protection Program. Either he skipped out on the feds or got spooked. Either way he might have come to Clovedale Falls looking for us. The question is *why*?”

“Isn’t it obvious? Joey stole millions from the DeVivos and testified against Vinnie DeVivo in court,” Rhonda replied. “Vinnie DeVivo was put away for life thanks to Joey's testimony.” Rhonda closed her eyes and saw the face of a deadly man enter her mind. “Frank DeVivo vowed to kill Joey and...us.”

“We were the ones who helped take down the DeVivo Family in Atlanta,” Rita pointed out. “We put Vinnie DeVivo behind bars for murder. We also help shut down Frank DeVivo's gambling and gun operations. Frank DeVivo vowed revenge on us the day his brother was sentenced to life in prison.”

Rhonda opened her eyes. “Joey gave the money he stole from the DeVivo Family over to the feds in exchange for protection,” she told Rita. “We both know that it can’t be Frank who killed Joey, though. Because a few months after Joey was safely tucked away in Witness Protection, Frank DeVivo was arrested for murder and sent off to prison.”

“I'll call Roger and see what's going on with Vinnie and Frank,” Rita told Rhonda and looked toward the kitchen, wringing her hands together. “Rhonda, if we don't get our bakery up and running--”

"Time is no longer on our side," Rhonda finished for Rita and looked toward the front door at a beautiful morning that now felt tainted instead of warm and cozy. "We have more to worry about than we bargained for."

Rita pulled up in front of the Peppermint Diner and parked her almost-new blue Dodge Crossroad Journey next to a run-down pickup truck. Other than the pickup truck and a white Jeep, the gravel parking lot was empty. "Well, you'll be happy to know that Roger assured me both Vinnie and Frank are still behind bars," she told Rhonda, parking the SUV. "He called the prison and spoke with a Warden Miller."

Rhonda glanced over at her twin sister. "If Vinnie and Frank are behind bars then who killed Joey?" she asked.

"I suppose it could still be unconnected to the DeVivo Family. But maybe Frank managed to reach Joey from inside the prison?" Rita suggested, feeling the cop inside of her speaking. "Frank could have organized a hit from inside the prison walls."

"Possibly," Rhonda agreed, turning her attention to the beautiful landscape surrounding the diner. The diner, painted like a large peppermint, sat at the side of a cozy road that hugged a gorgeous mountain river that ran deep in some places and shallow in other places. The river strolled through mountain land that was a beautiful picturesque site. “I'm starving. That bran muffin I ate for breakfast was lousy.”

“I'm hungry, too,” Rita agreed. She looked at the diner and let out a heavy sigh. “We've eaten here every day since we arrived in Clovedale Falls. Mrs. Widell is going to start thinking we can't cook for ourselves.”

“We can't,” Rhonda confessed. “Rita, we can bake cakes and cookies and pies and brownies but we can't cook dinner if our lives depend on it.”

“Years of eating take-out food, I'm afraid,” Rita pointed out in a sad voice. “Years of eating roadside barbecue on the go, or Chinese food on long stake-outs, years of rushing through drive-through windows on the way to work…”

“I get it, I get it,” Rhonda moaned. “I was there, remember? I practically spent my entire life savings in Mr. Chen's Chinese Restaurant. Mr. Chen was probably able to retire early because of me.”

Rita sighed. “I contributed a great deal of money to Mr. Chen, too,” she told Rhonda. “The only time we ever entered a kitchen was on our days off.”

“Baking was our way of relaxing,” Rhonda told Rita in a voice that seemed filled with sadness. “Sis?”

“Yes?”

“Did we do the right thing? Retiring, I mean?” Rhonda asked.

Rita turned her head in surprise and looked at Rhonda. "We both agreed the time had arrived."

"I know, I know," Rhonda replied, "but...boy, we sure had some good times, didn't we? On our days off we'd bake up a storm, wouldn't we? We'd just sit in my kitchen, drink coffee, and fill the kitchen full of cakes and pies and brownies."

Rita saw a warm kitchen still covered in sixties decor in her mind. Inside the kitchen she saw two women sitting at a round kitchen table sipping coffee and talking about getting married as the smell of delicious baking cakes wafted through the air. "We had many wonderful talks," she told Rhonda in a soft voice.

"We sure did," Rhonda agreed. She reached over and patted Rita's hand. "We still have many good talks ahead of us, too."

"I know," Rita said, forcing a smile to her face. "I know we do. But somehow...the talks will be different now. I never considered that when we retired."

"Did...we do the right thing by retiring?" Rhonda asked again. "I know we both were sick and tired of all the crime...the violence...just the plain ugliness of it all. But...well..."

"We were good cops," Rita finished for her sister.

Rhonda nodded. "We were good cops," she agreed. "We caught some real bad people, too."

"And made some real bad enemies in the process," Rita pointed out. "Vinnie and Frank DeVivo aren't the only ones who would like to see us swimming with the fishes."

"We never backed down from a fight and we never let the bad guys scare us," Rhonda replied forcing her voice to become stern. "Making enemies was all part of the job. We understood the risks and accepted them on a daily basis."

"Until...we almost died," Rita reminded Rhonda.

"That was beyond our control. That was nothing more than a stake-out gone real bad," Rhonda remembered, nodding as a heavy rain-consumed, eerie night came back to her mind. She saw a gray, unmarked cop car sitting outside of a run-down, closed carpet factory. Inside the factory a gun smuggling operation was at work. Rhonda and Rita were watching the factory, taking photos, gathering intelligence, and playing it easy while they waited for the FBI to get off their rear ends and get into the game. The FBI was holding Rhonda and Rita on a leash because the man in charge of the gun smuggling operation was the son of a popular politician. "We were marked," she told Rita in an upset voice. "The Feds left us out there to die."

"Yes, they did," Rita agreed, hearing the fateful gun shots that erupted through the front windshield of their unmarked cop car that night. She shuddered. "We barely escaped with our lives."

"Thanks to your quick thinking and skilled driving," Rhonda told Rita and patted her hand again.

Rita looked at Rhonda—looked deep into her sister's eyes.

"We did the right thing by retiring," she promised. "Police work has become political, Rhonda. A cop isn't serving an honest justice system anymore. Cops are just pawns sent to do the will of corrupt men and women and nothing more." Rita sighed. "Cops protect the guilty, Rhonda. We both understand this."

"You're right, Rita," Rhonda agreed. "But still...we managed to do some good. We managed to take drugs and guns off the streets and help some kids have a better chance at life. And to me that makes all the difference in the world."

Rita admired her sister's fighting spirit. "The time arrived, Rhonda, for us to leave the stage. Sure, we could have stayed on the force a while longer and fought for a few tidbits of justice, but you know as well as I do the mayor was glad to see us retire and leave the city. The old days, when being a cop mattered, are over with."

Rhonda felt sadness grip her heart. "I just...oh, you're right," she sighed. "I promised myself when we retired that I would accept our new adventure with hope, humor, and courage and not look back. But it's hard to keep that promise."

"You've been doing a good job so far."

"Up until we found Joey's body," Rhonda said with her eyes glued on the diner. "Joey always came to us for help, Rita. He must have come to Clovedale Falls to find us. Why? Who knows. But we need to find out."

"Which means risking placing our lives in danger again."

“We could already be in danger,” Rhonda pointed out.

“I'm not so sure,” Rita objected. “Whoever killed Joey could have easily killed us by now.” Rita bit down on her lip and thought for a few seconds. “Joey was poisoned.”

“Which means the killer wanted to keep his death silent,” Rhonda nodded.

“But why did the killer leave Joey's body in the open?” Rita asked. “Joey's body had to have been a message.”

“A warning. For us,” Rhonda agreed grimly, shaking her head. She nodded at the diner. “Let's go eat.”

Rita cautiously followed her sister out of the SUV. As she did, an old green truck pulled into the gravel parking lot and came to a stop very close to their SUV. “Rhonda--”

“My hand is already in my purse,” Rhonda promised Rita in a quiet voice and waited for the driver to exit the truck. When a chubby bellied man dressed like a backwoods farmer climbed out of the driver’s seat wearing a camouflage hunting hat with a fishhook stationed on the bill, Rhonda and Rita both sighed a breath of relief.

“Howdy,” Billy Northfield said in a thick Georgian accent. He waved at Rita and Rhonda with a large hand, his bright white teeth flashing in the sun as he offered a goofy but sincere smile.

“Your new husband,” Rhonda whispered to Rita in a teasing voice.

“Not funny,” Rita whispered back, taking in Billy's blue overalls covering a green short-sleeved shirt and his pair of old work boots. “Uh...hey,” she told Billy, moving her hand away from her purse. “Nice...day, isn't it?”

Billy glanced up at the clear blue sky. “Be raining before nightfall,” he said in a disappointed voice.

“The weather report isn't calling for any rain,” Rhonda told Billy.

Billy tossed his right thumb toward his old truck. Rita and Rhonda followed his thumb, looked at the truck, and spotted a Georgia Bloodhound sitting in the passenger's seat. The Bloodhound appeared lazy and bored, looking around at everything and nothing at the same time, with his tongue dangling free and lopsided out the side of his toothless mug. “Chester knows when it's going to rain,” Billy explained. “Whenever rain is coming, Chester gets in a foul mood. Why, just look at him...he's as grumpy as a mule stuck in a beehive.”

“He is?” Rhonda asked, staring at Chester. “Uh...how can you tell?”

“How can I tell?” Billy asked a shocked voice. “Chester ain't said a word to me all morning and barely touched his breakfast. Ornery is what he is. Ain't never seen a dog that don't like the rain. Chester takes the cake.”

“I see,” Rita said, looking at Chester. Chester glanced at her, flapped his right ear, and then went back to staring at a tree that held some unknown interest to him.

"See," Billy exclaimed and threw his hands up in the air, "every time Chester gets ornery he flaps that one ear." Billy looked at his truck. "I shouldn't bring you out any lunch...reckon I should, though!" he griped. Chester flapped his right ear again. "Don't give me no mouth or I'll bring you out a can of spinach!" Chester flapped his ear again. "Yeah, yeah," Billy drawled and threw his hand at Chester.

Rhonda looked at Billy and felt a smile touch her lips. The backwoods farmer, silly and obviously hamming it up for their benefit, was very sweet. "What's your name?" she asked.

Rita threw a panicked eye at her sister and shook her head no. "Don't," she begged in a desperate whisper.

"Oh, be nice," Rhonda whispered back.

Billy took his eyes off Chester and looked at Rhonda and Rita. My, he thought, the two women sure were pretty...and dressed real nice, too. And if he didn't know any better they were wearing the world's sweetest smelling perfume. That's when Billy realized he was dressed in his old field clothes and probably looked a mess...and smelled a mess, too. "My name is Billy Northfield. I own the Northfield Farm."

"The Northfield Farm?" Rita asked.

"Sure," Billy said and nodded his head proudly even though he felt a mess. "I grow all the pumpkins for the Pumpkin Festival, have a slew of apple orchards, and a whole bunch of other stuff." Billy glanced down at his overalls, quickly brushed off some dirt, and looked back up at Rita and Rhonda with a charming grin. “My great-great-granddaddy came to this part of the land years ago and started himself a small farm. Through the years my family has built the farm up into what it is today...buying a little more land here and there, adding this or that, planting this and that...it’s lots of hard work, but I’ve been used to it my whole life.” Billy sighed. “When my daddy passed away two years ago he left me and my sister the farm. My sister ain't much of a farmer...city gal, you know. She sold me her share of the farm and ain't looked back since. Better that way, too.” Billy looked around at the pristine hills reaching up to the horizon. “Both my folks are with the good Lord now and my sister, like I said, ain't much of a farmer. It's just me and Chester now.”

“Oh, that's sad,” Rhonda told Billy.

Billy looked at Rhonda, his eyes bashful. “Don't go feeling too sorry for me,” he told her. “I have my hands full with a whole bunch of people I hire to work my farm and the orchards. Gets to be that sometimes I can't catch a breath I keep so busy.”

“I’m sure your wife must be a big help.” When he looked away, embarrassed, Rhonda continued, “You're not married?” Rita let out a tiny, whispered moan.

“Was married once,” Billy told Rhonda. “Long time back. Wife up and left me after Daddy said he wasn't going to leave the farm to me because of her. I got real mad at Daddy, too...boy, did we ever have words. Daddy kept telling me my wife was poison but I just wouldn't listen.”

Billy sighed again. “Turns out Daddy was right on target. The woman I married was a money-hungry skunk...in the divorce her lawyer came out and said she was planning to convince me to sell the whole farm, so good riddance to her.” Billy glanced down at his chubby belly. “I didn't have this extra luggage back in those days,” he joked. “I'm forty-six years old...reckon it’s about time to carry around a spare tire.”

Rhonda smiled at Billy. The man was very sweet and honest, down to earth and real—real inside of his heart and soul. “My name is Rhonda Knight and this is my sister Rita Knight. We've just moved to Clovedale Falls.”

“Oh sure, the two cops from Atlanta,” Billy said. “I heard all about you.”

“Oh?” Rita asked, deciding to try and fish information out of Billy, “what did you hear?”

Billy fiddled with his hands for a second. “Folks like to talk is all,” he told Rita, feeling his cheeks turn red. “All I heard was that two retired sisters moved into town and bought Erma's old bakery. I reckon I was a bit surprised because everyone knows old Willy Matthews at the bank has it in for Erma and wasn't gonna let just anyone buy her bakery. My guess is when he found out you two were cops, he got smart and stopped playing games.”

“I guess so,” Rita said and offered Billy a polite smile. “Well, my sister and I are hungry and were just about to go inside and eat.” Rita looked at Rhonda, saw what her sister was thinking, sighed and said: “Uh, you're welcome to join us, Mr. Northfield. It would be nice to...get to know a neighbor."

"Just call me Billy," the man beamed. He couldn't believe two beautiful women were asking him to eat lunch with them. Boy, what a beautiful day. "I'd be mighty happy to eat lunch with you. Mrs. Widell has the best food in town."

Rhonda gave Rita a loving eye and followed after Billy, who held the door open for the two sisters like the proper gentleman his folks had raised him to be.

As the trio stepped into the diner, a black car slowly crawled down the road, stopped in front of the diner, and then crept away, unseen and unheard.

"Yes, sir," Billy told Rita and Rhonda, plopping down at a booth with pink-red-and-white striped vinyl seats like a peppermint candy, "Mrs. Widell has the best food in town."

Rita sat down next to Rhonda and smelled the air. The air smelled of fresh, hot coffee, apple pie and chicken and dumplings. *We'll forget our troubles during lunch,* she thought, *and just enjoy a delicious meal with a strange...silly...new friend, because anything might happen after lunch.*

3

Brenda Widell walked up to the booth where Rita and Rhonda sat with Billy, carrying a red and white wooden tray laden with three peppermint candy-themed mugs filled with hot coffee. "I was wondering when you girls were going to run into our Billy," she said in a raspy voice caused by years of smoking cigarettes. Fortunately, at the age of sixty-five, Brenda had finally kicked the habit, replacing her cigarettes with butterscotch candy. She sucked on a butterscotch as she set down their coffees and whipped out her order pad from the pocket of her apron.

Billy took his coffee and smiled. "Daddy always did say you were one of the smartest women in town. And a mighty pretty woman, at that."

Brenda rolled her eyes. "Your Daddy, God rest his soul, said silly things ever since he and I were kids in grade school together. Besides, I have to dye my hair red these days, my face has more wrinkles than I can count, I'm wearing the same old red and white uniform dress I always wear, and I'm constipated. So don't try to sweet-talk a free slice of apple pie out of me, Billy Northfield." Brenda set down a fresh pitcher of cream for their coffee and gave the women a significant look. "Billy always tries to sweet-talk a free slice of pie out of me."

Rhonda smiled. Even though her mind was worried she felt her humor slowly wake up. "Maybe he just likes peppermint?" she joked.

Rita nudged Rhonda with her elbow. "Don't start," she begged.

"I was only joking," Rhonda promised and winked at Brenda. "You do look very lovely."

"Aw, I'm nothing but myself, girls, and happy to be myself," Brenda drawled with wise finality. She turned her attention back to Billy. "Haven't seen you in a while."

"You know how busy I am this time of year," Billy explained. "Getting the tractors ready for the hayrides, getting the pumpkins prepared, the cider house ready, the apples picked, washed and bagged...ain't hardly had time to catch my breath."

"Well," Brenda told Billy, "you complain every year about being busy but you always get ready in time and make a lot of folks happy. Next year you'll be sitting in this same booth complaining my ears off again and I'll tell you the same thing."

Billy felt his cheeks turn red. “I reckon I do complain this time of year, don't I?” he asked with a grin.

Brenda nodded. “Right on time, like clockwork.” Brenda winked at Rita and Rhonda. “Wouldn't have it any other way, either. Now, I'm cooking up my special chicken and dumplings for lunch along with okra, cream corn, fresh biscuits, and apple pie. I'll bring out your plates after you've worked on your coffee for a bit.”

“Sounds good,” Billy smiled and glanced around the diner. “Folks will start pouring in here soon. Nice to have the place to ourselves for a few minutes.”

“Oh, I doubt I'll do much business today,” Brenda told Billy.

“How come?” Billy asked.

“Haven't you heard?”

“Heard what?” Billy asked in a confused voice. “I've been out on the tractor all morning.”

“My,” Brenda said, “news sure does reach your farm slower and slower these days.”

“Brenda, what in the world are you talking about?” Billy insisted. Rita and Rhonda tensed up.

“Why, there's been a murder in town,” Brenda told Billy in a low whisper. “Some stranger was found dead in poor Lilly's shop. Rumor is he was shot ten times.”

“Ten times?” Billy exclaimed.

"No...no," Rhonda protested before she could catch herself, "that man was poisoned--" Rhonda caught her mouth when she saw the big, round eyes of Brenda and Billy staring at her. "Oh dear."

"Oh," Brenda said in a gossipy voice, "I should have known you two would be involved." Brenda scooted in next to Billy. "Spill the beans and don't let the pot boil dry."

Rita gave Rhonda an upset look. "Mrs. Widell, I really can't--"

"It's Brenda," the waitress told Rita in a stern but caring voice. "Miss Rita Knight, how many times have I told you to call me Brenda?"

Rita eased her purse off the table and placed it next to her leg. "Brenda...I'm sorry, but my sister and I don't know anything," she explained. "We were in our bakery speaking with Mrs. Wilson when Mrs. DeLoach came running inside and told us about the body. My sister and I did go investigate. We did find a body, but that's all we did. We can't say any more than that."

"They have been coming in here for awhile so Brenda knows," Rhonda jumped in, hoping to help Rita. "Sheriff Bluestone is the law here, not us, and we respect that." Rhonda looked down at her coffee and then back up at Brenda. "We decided it was time to start living a quiet, peaceful life in a nice little town like Clovedale Falls."

Brenda studied Rhonda's eyes. "Honey," she said, "I raised four daughters who tried to throw every trick in the book at me. None of their tricks ever worked, either. So don't try to pull a fast one on old Brenda Widell because she knows backdoor talk when she hears it."

Rhonda winced. She was used to dealing with city people who spoke fancy words and pretended to be a lot smarter than they really were. In Clovedale Falls she had expected to encounter small town folks with simple minds. Instead she was finding out that the small town folks she encountered—even though they spoke in simple, homegrown ways—were far smarter than the city people she had battled with most of her life. "Brenda, I'm being honest," she promised.

"On one level...but you're also hiding something from us," Brenda pointed out.

Rita tensed again. The last thing she needed—or wanted—was for a woman like Brenda to meddle in business that wasn't any of her concern. Sure, Brenda was a nice woman, caring and warm, but she also was a woman who needed to learn boundaries. The last thing Rhonda and Rita needed was to get on the sheriff's bad side for spreading around gossip about the crime scene that might mess up his investigative process. "A man was found dead. Sheriff Bluestone informed us that Doc Downing believes the man was poisoned. That's all we know," she said in a voice that set Brenda back a few paces.

"I see," Brenda said and slowly stood up. "Well, if that's all you know...I better go check on your food."

Rhonda watched Brenda wander away toward a wooden front counter with a red Formica top and bright chrome around the edges. Rhonda nudged Rita in the side. “Did you have to be rude?” she asked.

“I'm afraid so,” Rita confirmed. “And you should understand why.”

“Should I go?” Billy asked, seeing Rita's eyes turn fierce with aggravation.

“No, no,” Rhonda told Billy and quickly patted Rita's hand. “Well...yes, I suppose you should. My sister and I need to talk.”

“I'll go eat up at the front counter,” Billy told Rhonda and quickly stood up. “It was nice meeting you.” He raised the bill of his hat briefly toward them, as if tipping an old fashioned top hat to them both. “If you get a chance, come by my farm and I'll give you girls a free hayride and some pumpkins.”

“That sounds lovely,” Rhonda promised Billy and offered him a warm smile. “My sister and I are very grateful for your kindness, Mr. Northfield...I mean...Billy. We'll visit your farm the first chance we get.”

“You better get your bakery in order first,” Billy pointed out. “Pumpkin Festival is right on top of us and you girls ain't got a whole bunch of time to get Erma's old bakery in order. Better hurry because this town depends on outside folks to keep going.”

"Don't remind us," Rita moaned and plopped her face down in her hands.

"Did I say something wrong?" Billy asked.

"Oh no," Rhonda promised and slid around to Billy's seat. "My sister and I just feel...overwhelmed, that's all."

"I understand," Billy replied in a polite voice, tipped his hat once more, and turned away politely to walk to the front counter.

"I was rude, wasn't I?" Rita asked quietly.

"Yes, you were," Rhonda said.

"I'll apologize to Brenda when she comes back out," Rita promised. "And maybe to Billy, too." She raised her head and looked at Rhonda. "Word is out that there has been a murder. A lot of people are going to start looking in our direction and asking questions. We don't have time to serve as gossip hounds for a bunch of bored, small-town people who have nothing better to do than reread the morning paper over and over again." She crossed her arms over her chest in exasperation.

"That's not very nice," Rhonda chided her sister.

Rhonda lowered her coffee. "I don't like walking around in the dark no more than you do, but at the moment...what choice do we have? All we can do is keep searching for answers--"

"All we need to be doing is preparing our bakery for opening day," Rita informed Rhonda. "However, the cop in me understands that if we leave Joey's death untouched we could be placing our lives in danger." Rita took another sip of coffee, thinking. "Roger is up to his ears in work. He can't offer us much help right now. He barely had the time to investigate Vinnie and Frank DeVivo for us."

"Roger works for the fraud division anyway," Rhonda replied. "When it comes to money, the government wants immediate justice. What can you do except please the politicians demanding their gold?"

Rita ignored this little bit of commentary and kept thinking on the problem. "I could contact Nathan," Rita offered.

"No way," Rhonda objected in a desperate voice. "Nathan Miles is the world's biggest jerk, not to mention he's the world's biggest moron." Rhonda rolled her eyes. "The guys think he's Dick Tracy or something."

"Nathan does work with Homicide," Rita pointed out. "And he was very fond of us."

"He was fond of our faces," Rhonda corrected Rita. "Nathan would flirt with a two-ton circus woman if she had a pretty face."

"I suppose you're right," Rita agreed and sipped her coffee. "There's Paula--"

"Paula Young would sell out her own mother for a donut," Rhonda interrupted. "The woman is a power-hungry nut who puts the lives of innocent people in danger."

"How about Stacey Ruppert?"

"Stacey Ruppert is even worse than Paula Young," Rhonda replied. "Let's face it, Rita, all the good cops we used to know are gone. The people that worked Homicide with us are nothing but a bunch of heartless animals thirsting for power. Roger was the only good guy left."

Rita sighed. "The mayor did get rid of all the good cops, didn't she?"

"Including us," Rhonda nodded. "In her own corrupt way, that is."

"Instead of words she used resistance, replacing our department with new faces that became strangers to us. Only Nathan, Paula, and Stacey were left--"

"Three jerks who I never trusted."

"Jerks or not, we worked with them for five years before we retired," Rita pointed out. "They weren't completely incompetent. They were our colleagues."

"In the old days that might have meant something, but to a bunch of young thirty-year-old know-it-all kids...nothing."

"Rhonda, we need help. I know I'm grasping at the bottom of the barrel here, but we (are) coming up empty-handed. What do you want me to do?"

"Calling three people who I never trusted isn't the answer," Rhonda said in a stern voice.

Rita put down her coffee. She felt frustrated but knew her sister was right. "You're right," she said. "The only person

I trust is Roger. I shouldn't have brought up Nathan, Paula, and Stacey. Those three are...very untrustworthy."

"You're upset and frustrated."

"Yes, that's true," Rita agreed, "but I can't let my common sense become dull." Rita looked around the diner. "If Roger can't be of any help right now, I suppose the only choice we have is to speak with Sheriff Bluestone and confess the truth to him and ask to be allowed to help investigate the murder ourselves."

"We're not cops anymore."

"Is that the part that matters?" Rita asked.

Rhonda looked down at her hands for a long time. "We know the background about Joey. After lunch we'll go speak with the Sheriff. I wanted to use absolute caution...but a little part of me feels that the sheriff can be trusted. I guess we'll find out in time."

"I feel that he is an honest man," Rita told Rhonda. "He's from the old days who still lives by his code of honor." Rita looked into Rhonda's eyes with deep care. "We should have honored our own code of honor and told him the truth instead of running away like a couple of scared little girls."

"I'm still not going to give the man my diary, either. Joey is dead, Rita, and we need answers. But I'd rather keep the investigation small. Roger is barely hanging on by the tips of his fingers. Regardless of what people believe, we retired cops don't have a phonebook full of names to call when we're in a pinch."

"The only option we have is to make friends with the sheriff and hope he invites us on board…and pray he turns out to be a friend and not an enemy."

"Speaking of friends," Rhonda said, "before we leave, you need to make up with Brenda. If we're going to survive in this town we can't afford to offend the locals, Rita."

Rita agreed. She looked up at movement across the diner. "Speaking of Brenda, there she is now."

Rhonda looked over her shoulder and spotted Brenda carrying two red and white plates full of delicious food. "Make it sweet," she begged Rita.

"I will," Rita promised.

"Here you go, girls," Brenda said in a warm but careful voice and carefully set the plates down.

Rita drew in a deep breath. "Brenda, please forgive me for being rude earlier," she said in a sincere voice. "I've been very upset this morning and I had no right to be rude to you. I understand if you want us to leave and never come back."

Brenda looked down at Rita, read the distress in her eyes, and then gently touched the woman's face with a loving hand. "Honey," she said, "you weren't being rude with me," she promised. "You were fussing at whatever you're hiding. A blind bat could see that. Now, eat your lunch and relax because there's nothing in the world you can do or say to ever make me hate you."

Rita nodded and sat in shock. Rhonda nearly broke out in tears of happiness. Billy just smiled. Small-town folk were sure a lot different than city folk.

Brad invited Rita and Rhonda into a small office that resembled a remote hunting lodge somewhere deep in the mountains of Alaska. The office smelled of cherry tobacco that made Rita and Rhonda feel cozy inside even though they had come to discuss murder. “Sit down,” Brad said and pointed at two brown cushioned chairs sitting in front of a worn-down wooden desk that was immaculately organized. Brad was obviously not a slob.

“Thank you,” Rita said in a polite voice and took the left sitting chair. Rhonda parked herself in the right chair and gave Rita a cautious eye. Rita nodded. “Sheriff Bluestone--”

“Call me Brad,” he said, planting himself behind his desk and picking up a coffee mug. “Strangers call me Sheriff Bluestone. Or Sheriff Rawhide, behind my back,” he chuckled. “We're going to be neighbors, so call me Brad, ladies, if you please.”

“Okay...Brad,” Rita said and carefully eased forward. “My sister and I know the man who was killed.”

“I know,” Brad said and took a drink of coffee. “I read your faces.”

Rhonda looked into Brad's eyes with surprise and saw a good, honest man that she wanted to trust—who she needed to trust. Yet she hesitated. “Joey 'The Bookie' Stally is the man who was killed,” she told Brad. “My sister and I helped Joey avoid a serious prison sentence in return for his very powerful testimony against a crime family we were trying to take down at the time.”

“Joey Stally helped you ladies put Vinnie DeVivo behind bars for life,” Brad told Rhonda. “I've been doing some investigating and made a few calls. It didn't take me long to connect the man to you two ladies.” Brad took another drink of coffee. “You two did some fine work. From what I found out Vinnie DeVivo was a deadly snake who hurt a lot of people.”

Rita and Rhonda glanced at each other, impressed by the sheriff's sharp assessment of the situation. “Vinnie DeVivo was a slime ball,” Rhonda agreed.

“Joey Stally wasn't much better,” Brad pointed out.

“No, Joey wasn't a saint,” Rita agreed, walking into a police room in her mind. She snatched up a cold file, grabbed a cup of coffee, and plopped down behind a desk, reminiscing about every detail from his case. “Joey stole a lot of money from the DeVivo Family. He stole ten percent from every bet clients paid out to them. When Vinnie DeVivo finally found out that Joey was skimming off the top of the bets, he set out to kill him.”

“Only Joey had witnessed Vinnie kill a man name Chuck Langston, a very dangerous drug dealer who had already betrayed Vinnie," Rhonda continued. "Chuck Langston was also one of Joey's biggest gambling clients."

"Chuck Langston was connected to the Street Coyotes," Rita told Brad. "The Street Coyotes were...and still are...a vicious biker gang that has outposts in Atlanta, Miami, Los Angeles, Las Vegas--"

"And Phoenix," Brad finished for Rita. "I'm aware of the Street Coyotes. Those skunks have caused some damage in Phoenix. The feds are having a hard time putting them on a leash."

Rhonda nodded. "When Vinnie killed Chuck Langston, a man named Lewis Stevens went mad with rage. Vinnie DeVivo, even though he was a tough guy, wet his pants and changed his mind about killing Joey. Or maybe he just thought he could kill two birds with one stone and decided to pin Chuck Langston's murder on Joey instead, hoping Lewis Stevens would do away with Joey and leave Vinnie's hands clean. In a manner of speaking."

"That's when Joey came to us," Rita told Brad. "We were already riding Joey's back, believing he killed Chuck Langston, but didn't have enough proof to arrest him. When Joey came to us claiming he had proof that Vinnie DeVivo killed Chuck Langston, well, you can imagine our surprise."

"But Joey was telling the truth," Rhonda told Brad. "Joey was hiding in the alley that Vinnie killed Chuck Langston in. The guy actually had a tape recorder on him and recorded Chuck begging for his life. He knew at the time that Vinnie was mad as hell and might try to pin it on him later. Turned out to be a smart move."

"Joey recorded every conversation he had with his clients," Rita said. "Joey might have been a slime but he was a clever and cautious criminal who knew how to watch his back."

Brad worked on his coffee for a second and then nodded his head. "And then Joey Stally was put in the Witness Protection Program after he testified in court."

"Yes, he was," Rita agreed. "Maybe you can tell us why Joey came here. Did he leave the Witness Protection Program?"

Brad put down his coffee. "The FBI agent I spoke to an hour ago told me Joey Stally went missing from his assigned location about two weeks ago. Once he leaves his assigned protection, he's considered out of Witness Protection for good."

Rita and Rhonda changed worried glances. "We thought the DeVivo Family killed Joey...assuming maybe Frank DeVivo, Vinnie's brother, managed to send out a hit on Joey from inside the prison." Rita paused then carefully moved forward. "A friend of ours has assured us that both Vinnie and Frank DeVivo are still behind prison bars. That doesn't mean Frank, or even Vinnie, couldn't have reached Joey from inside the prison."

"Frank DeVivo did vow to kill Joey, after all...and to kill the two women sitting in your office," Rhonda told Brad in a very cautious voice. If Brad wasn't as trustworthy as he appeared, she had just given the man dangerous ammunition to attack with.

Brad folded his arms together. “Could it be that Lewis Stevens is still seeking revenge for Chuck Langston’s death and he’s the one who got to Joey Stally?” he asked. “I checked and that rat Stevens is still running free out in Los Angeles.”

“Why would Lewis Stevens kill Joey?” Rhonda asked. “Joey helped convict the man Lewis Stevens wanted dead. It was proved in court that it was Vinnie and not Joey.”

Brad shrugged his shoulders, musing. “Maybe he didn’t believe it. Just an idea,” he said and then moved on. “Doc Downing sent the body off to the state crime lab for an autopsy. It'll be at least two days before we get the results. In the meantime, the big boys down in Atlanta have shown no interest in peeking their heads in Clovedale Falls. As a matter of fact, the FBI agent I talked to seemed relieved that Joey Stally was dead.” Brad unfolded his arms, picked up his coffee, took a sip, and then said: “Joey Stally was tracked here as easy as a desert rat running in the open from a snake. I think you two ladies know that.”

“Yes,” Rita said, and the two sisters exchanged a grim look. “What we don't understand, or know, is why Joey came to Clovedale Falls at all. Our communication with him ended the day he testified in court.”

Brad nodded his head. “That's the mystery here,” he agreed and then asked: “Did the feds recover the money

Joey Stally skimmed off the top from the DeVivo Family deals?"

"Yes, Joey turned over the money in exchange for protection," Rita explained. "That was part of the deal he made with the prosecutor. His testimony alone wasn't enough to satisfy the feds. Joey had to turn over the money or be denied protection."

"To be honest," Rhonda added, "after Joey testified in court against Vinnie DeVivo, we didn't care...we didn't care what the feds did with him. We washed our hands of the man and moved on. You know how it is, I'm sure. It was on to the next case for us."

Brad finished off his coffee and looked across his office at a window covered with a thick wooden blind. The blind was pulled open, allowing the afternoon's beautiful sunlight to flood into the small office. He spotted a few falling leaves playing in the crisp air outside and focused his thoughts before he asked his next question. "Could it be that Joey Stally didn't turn over all the money he stole from the DeVivo Family after all?"

"It's possible," Rhonda agreed. "But the question we need to focus on is why Joey came to Clovedale Falls. The simplest explanation is that he was trying to find my sister and me. The question is why? As I told you, we washed our hands of him after he testified in court."

"Why would Joey try to locate two cops who had nothing else to offer him?" Rita asked.

Brad rubbed his chin. "The man obviously found out you

two were retired, which means he had to have made a few phone calls."

"We thought about that over lunch," Rhonda told Brad.

"Or maybe," Brad suggested as a new thought occurred to him, "somebody made it too easy for Joey Stally to locate you."

"Are you talking about an insider?" Rita asked.

Brad shrugged his shoulders. "Not sure," he told Rita. "All I know right now is that whoever killed Joey Stally was a professional killer. You ladies know that as well."

"We...know," Rhonda confessed in a worried voice. "No stranger comes to town and gets killed with poison. If it was a crime of passion it would have been a gun or a knife. What we don't know is why the killer left Joey's body in the candle shop."

"We're assuming it was a message...a message to get our attention," Rita told Brad as fear and frustration built up in her chest and her cheeks turned pink. "I feel like I'm chasing my tail," she complained. "We're asking questions and have no answers."

"That's true," Brad pointed out, "but at least you came to me for help." Brad leaned forward. "I'm going to stand by you, ladies," he promised in a stern and caring voice. "I can tell by your faces that you're wary about trusting me, and I'm not asking for your trust...not yet. All I'm asking you is to put back on your badges and help me solve this case."

"But...-we are retired," Rita stated. "We have a bakery to get in order before the festival starts. We have so much work to do. We can't involve ourselves in a murder case. If we miss the festival we'll be financially sunk. My sister and I have invested a great deal of money, effort...and hope...into the bakery, our new home, and this town."

Brad understood Rita's anger and desperation. The Pumpkin Festival kept Clovedale Falls chugging along. Folks who missed that train quickly sank down into bankruptcy. The last thing Brad wanted to see was for Rita and Rhonda to fail. However, being a cop came first—justice came first—and commitment to duty came first. "Ladies," he said in a careful voice, "my guys are small-town guys who aren't trained to solve homicides. My guys are simple family men who write out speeding tickets and handle the school crossings. At the most they'll tangle with a drunk here and there or arrest a trouble maker or chase down some rowdy kids." Brad studied Rita and Rhonda's eyes. "I need experienced cops on the case and what I've learned about you two over the last few hours is enough to convince me that you're what I need."

"We don't have much of a case," Rhonda told Brad.

Brad leaned back in his chair. "You two ladies didn't come here to ask me to keep you behind a desk."

"No, we didn't," Rita confessed. She drew in a deep breath and steadied her worried mind. "Sheriff...Brad...my sister and I have financial obligations that must be met. We have a bakery to open and a health inspection to pass." Rita calmly placed her hands down onto her lap. "Whoever killed Joey could still be in town, waiting to see how my sister and I react. Isn't that a bigger problem? Until we get to the bottom of this case we won't be able to commit ourselves to the bakery."

"Looking over your shoulder every second isn't good for business," Rhonda jumped in.

Brad nodded his head. "I wouldn't think it would be," he agreed.

Rita looked at Rhonda, studied her sister's face, and then focused back on Brad. "For the time being, if you will allow, my sister and I would like to join the investigation, with your approval."

Brad nodded his head again, snatched open the top right drawer of his desk, and snatched out two badges. "I'll swear you in myself," he said in a proud voice.

Rhonda stared at the two badges Brad held out to them and felt a strange sensation wash through her heart. "We moved here to start a new chapter," she told Brad. "I never assumed...I would be a cop again. Once they sent me my retirement papers..."

"I know what you mean," Brad told Rhonda. "When I started drawing my pension I felt like my entire world had come to a halt. I felt like an outsider...a stranger to myself." Brad slid the two badges across the desk. "We never stop being cops, ladies, just like the tiger can't change his stripes. Being a cop is who we are."

Rita reached out for her badge but then paused. “I want to stop being a cop when we’re done, though,” she told Brad. “I want to bake cakes and cookies and sit in my kitchen drinking coffee on rainy days. I want to explore the small grocery store in town and make new friends. I want to drink apple cider as autumn leaves fall all around me. I want to explore corn mazes and make pumpkin pies and go on hayrides.” Rita looked up at Brad. “My sister and I served twenty years as cops,” she said. “That was long enough.”

Rhonda carefully picked up her badge. “Rita, we won't have peace until we solve this case,” she said in a regretful voice. “It's just for a short while. I want the same things you want, but right now we have work to do.”

Rita drew in a deep breath, picked up her badge, placed it down into her purse, and stood up. “Where's the coffee station and donuts?” she asked.

Rhonda let out a sigh of relief. “I thought I was supposed to be the funny one?”

“I'm not trying to be funny,” Rita pointed out. “I really want a cup of coffee and a donut. If I'm going to start being a cop again I want to start off on the right foot.”

Brad grinned. “Coffee station is in the front room. Donuts might be a bit stale.”

“What else is new,” Rita complained and walked out of Brad's office. He chuckled good-naturedly.

“My sister...can be difficult at times,” Rhonda told Brad. “But she's a good cop and she's also my best friend. So please, go easy on her.”

Brad stood up. “Good cops are always rough around the edges,” he told Rhonda. “The only thing I'm worried about is remembering which one of you is Rita Knight and which one of you is Rhonda Knight.” And with those words Brad smiled and walked Rhonda out into the front room where they found Rita pouring herself a cup of coffee. He promised to make a few phone calls and alert them when it was time for them to take the next step with the investigation.

Outside, the same black car that drove past the diner eased past the sheriff's office like a snake slithering through the shadows, stalking its prey, ready to devour its next victim.

4

Rita strolled out onto a sidewalk decorated with haystacks mingled with pumpkins. The sights, smells, and sensations of autumn surrounded her in every direction. Every sidewalk, storefront, and tree was decorated with fall foliage. The decorations weren't shabby or corny—they were all handmade, created with love and care, and framed the season with perfect brilliance. Clovedale Falls was dressed and ready. "It's very lovely," Rita told Rhonda as a breeze lifted her hair up off her shoulders. "I fell in love with this little town the first time we visited. It's a shame that this beautiful day is being ruined by a murder."

Rhonda looked across the street and spotted the Peppermint Coffee Shop, an easy walk for bored deputies in need of fresh coffee and donuts. A hand-carved wooden sign stood outside the front door of the coffee shop: an oversized cup of coffee painted red and white, with a little boy dressed in a winter coat standing next to it. The little boy was smiling and pointing at the cup of coffee. “Rita, Joey's death hasn't ended our lives. We're going to solve this case and get our bakery open...and who knows, maybe I'll put up some more smiley face stickers?”

“Not on your life,” Rita replied and rolled her eyes. “One sticker on the cash register is enough.”

“We'll see,” Rhonda managed to tease her sister. “Now, let's get back to our bakery and see what we can do. We can’t do anything with the investigation until Brad calls us back, but we have about four hours before we have to be at Erma's for dinner. That should give us enough time to at least get the old appliances out of the kitchen and into the back alley. Tomorrow we'll rent a truck and haul the appliances off.”

Rita agreed. “I guess you’re right. There isn't much we can do right now,” she said. “Brad is burning up the phone lines for us and there's no sense in crowding his office.”

“No, there isn't,” Rhonda told Rita, forcing her voice to sound positive. “Brad said he will call or drop by the bakery if he finds out anything. In the meantime, there's no point in letting good work hours go to waste.” Rhonda drew in a deep breath and walked her eyes up and down the street. A few people—mostly elderly or retired folks—were out and about, strolling here and there, enjoying the afternoon. What Rhonda didn't see was any sign of a threat. Yet her gut told her that whoever killed Joey Stally was hiding in Clovedale Falls; she knew Rita felt the same threat. But threat or no threat, Rhonda wasn't about to cower and hide her head in the sand. Clovedale Falls was her home and she wasn't about to run scared. “Ready?” she asked Rita.

Rita looked around. “Rhonda?” she asked.

“Yes?”

“If this were the old days and cops were still cops...would we have really retired? I mean, if cops were still like Brad?” Rita asked.

“I doubt it,” Rhonda confessed. “We retired because times changed on us...people changed us...and justice betrayed us. When a cop can't trust another cop, it's time to throw in the towel.”

Rita put her eyes on Rhonda. “Brad is a good man,” she said in a thoughtful voice. “I feel that we can trust him with our lives. And it's men like Brad that made me want to become a cop to begin with...men who stand for truth, honor, and justice. Men who don't back down from a fight.” Rita looked down at her purse. “I feel we did back down from a fight when we retired.”

Rhonda understood what her sister was feeling. “Rita, when we first became cops times were different. We became cops when the world began to take a serious nose dive.” Rhonda looked around, watching an old man carrying a newspaper as he entered the coffee shop; next to him a younger woman passed by staring into her mobile phone, almost tripping over the sidewalk in front of her. Rhonda sighed. “People have changed,” she said. “Little towns like Clovedale Falls are the last strongholds for people who still want to live normal, decent lives. Big cities have become polluted crime centers run by criminals dressed up like politicians. Sure, we might have thrown in the towel, but we had good reason to."

"Sometimes," Rita said, "I think about the children...my mind goes back to the drug infested neighborhood we helped clean up. I think about those children sitting in doorways, scared to come outside and play because drug dealers are standing on every street corner with guns. I think about their hungry faces. And then I think about what we helped that neighborhood become." Rita smiled. "We helped get the drug dealers out, clean the streets, put a playground in, and really make a difference."

"We did make a difference," Rhonda promised. "But it's up to people to make the difference. People matter." Rhonda motioned around with her hands. "Now it's time to make a difference in Clovedale Falls. We have to focus on our town and let the outside world go on destroying itself, if it really wants to."

"Boy," Rita said, "if Dad could hear us talking now he'd swear we weren't his daughters."

Rhonda laughed. "Tell me about it," she said and looked at Rita. "When did we become adults?"

Rita shrugged her shoulders. "Time has a tendency to fly when you least expect it," she replied and drew in another breath of fresh, cool air. "Rhonda?"

"Yes?"

Rita looked around. “I want to be happy in this quaint little town and forget about my former life, once this investigation is over. I’m serious. I want to begin a new life and be happy.”

“You will be,” Rhonda promised.

Rita bit down on her lower lip. “I know I've been a little on edge about our finances, and I'm sorry. I only want everything to go right for us. I want our bakery to be a grand success and...I want our lives to be filled with peace and happiness.” Rita looked at her sister with love. “You're all I have and I never want to see you hurt or disappointed. I never want to be hurt or disappointed, either.” Rita drew in a deep breath. “I guess what I'm trying to say is that I'm very scared that failure might be our fate and if that happens we might have to leave Clovedale Falls and return back to the ugliness we thought we escaped for good. I honestly don't think I could stand that.”

Rhonda reached out her hands and put them on Rita's shoulders. “Rita, listen to me,” she said in a caring voice, “we're not going to fail, do you hear me? People said we wouldn't last a day in the Navy and we did. People said there was no way we would ever become cops and we did. We always accomplish what is in our hearts, don't we?”

“Well...yes.”

“And we manage to do so not just because we are stubborn goats but because we have faith in the Lord,” Rhonda continued. “It's always been our belief that God will put us where we need to be in life.” Rhonda smiled. “We're not going to fail, Rita, I promise. We're going to grow old in our bakery and live in our cabin until it falls down to the ground."

Rita stared into her sister's loving eyes and felt a hopeful smile touch her lips. "Promise?"

"You bet I promise," Rhonda smiled. "Now let's--" Rhonda stopped speaking when she spotted a black car turn the corner of Turtle Dove Lane and slowly begin driving toward the sheriff's office. "Rita--"

"My hand is already in my purse," Rita assured. She locked her eyes on the car and cautiously eased Rhonda toward the hood of her SUV. "Be prepared to drop and start shooting."

"I'm ready," Rhonda assured Rita as she stuck her hand inside of her purse and wrapped it around the grip of her gun.

The black car drove up to Rita's SUV and stopped. Rita and Rhonda waited. A few seconds later the back door opened and a man who appeared to be in his early seventies appeared. "Valentine DeVivo," Rhonda whispered.

Rita felt fear grip her heart. "Stay calm," she whispered.

Valentine DeVivo calmly smoothed out his expensive black suit and then ran his hands through his thick gray hair. "Nice day," he said in a thickly accented voice. His Sicilian accent was so heavy there were twice as many vowels in every word when he spoke, and it was unmistakable to the Knight sisters, who knew his crime family too well.

Rita and Rhonda watched Valentine reach into his right pocket, retrieve a pair of black shades, and slide them over his eyes with hands that were wrinkled but still extremely powerful. "Valentine DeVivo isn't allowed in the country," Rhonda whispered to Rita. "Vinnie and Frank took over for him. Too many warrants out for his name."

"I know," Rita whispered back.

"Oh yeah, you do," Rhonda said, watching Valentine look around with ease and confidence. She shuddered.

"We should talk," Valentine called out in a relaxed voice. "We should walk and talk."

Rita glanced at Rhonda. Rhonda nodded. "What at do you want, Mr. DeVivo?" she called out in a careful voice.

"Is a very nice day, no?" Valentine said again. "We should walk and talk on a fine day like this." Valentine snapped his right fingers at the black car. "Go park and get food. Be back in one hour."

To Rita and Rhonda's relief, the black car drove away. "What do we have to losc?" Rhonda asked and removed her hand from her purse. Rita studied Valentine and then followed her sister. "Okay, Mr. Valentine, let's walk and talk."

Valentine looked at Rhonda and then placed his eyes on Rita. "We walk and talk in peace," he pointed out, eyes flickering to their purses only briefly. “My days of being a hard man are finished.”

“Are they?” Rita asked.

Valentine nodded his head. “Yes,” he said and pointed down the street. As he started in that direction, he stopped. Then pointed at Rhonda. “Only you. Your sister can stay here. If we don't return in one hour she can release the dogs on me.”

“No deal,” Rita objected.

Rhonda looked around. “Rita, I'll be okay,” she promised.

“No deal,” Rita confirmed. “I'll walk behind you.”

Valentine shrugged his shoulders. “Good enough,” he said and began walking.

“I'll stay close,” Rita promised Rhonda.

“I know you will,” Rhonda replied, gave Rita a quick hug, and caught up to Valentine. “Okay, Mr. DeVivo, what do you want to talk about? I'm sure you’re not here because you're interested in the Pumpkin Festival.”

“Can't an old man enjoy this little town, all the sights and sounds others enjoy?” Valentine asked.

“Depends on who that old man is.”

Valentine clasped his hands behind his back. “I admit my reputation sometimes make people to become – how you say – worried. Alarmed,” he said. “My younger years were not very clean.”

"You murdered people and stole from the poor," Rhonda pointed out. "You're wanted on at least a dozen Interpol warrants."

Valentine didn't deny the accusations Rhonda threw at him. "I was a monster, yes," he agreed. "Very horrible things."

Rhonda glanced over at Valentine. To her shock, she saw an old man filled with sorrow for the life he had once lived. "What do you want, Mr. DeVivo? Why did you want to talk?"

"Joseph Stally was killed," Valentine said in an open voice. "Joey Stally, as you know him. Unless I find out the killer, my two sons also will be killed."

"Oh?" Rhonda asked. She turned this over in her mind, trying to search his tone for lies.

Valentine walked past a candy shop, stopped, studied a display window full of delicious peppermint fudge, and then looked at Rhonda. "Joey stole millions from the family. He skimmed off the earnings for decades. As you maybe guess, he only gave up a small slice of the pie and hid away the rest for later." He gave a wan smile and looked sad.

Rhonda glanced over her shoulder at Rita. Rita waited at a respectful distance. "What does any of this have to do with me and my sister?" she asked.

Valentine focused his eyes back on the peppermint fudge. "I was hoping you could tell me," he said in a low voice.

“Mr. DeVivo, my sister, and I have no idea why Joey Stally came to Clovedale Falls. All we do know is that he was poisoned.”

Valentine grew silent. He stared at the peppermint fudge for a long time. When he spoke, his voice was very careful. “If I do not find who is killer of Joey Stally, my two sons also will die.” Valentine shifted his eyes over to Rhonda. “There is...a person...he say that my two sons, they know where is this money Joey stole from me.”

“Do they?”

“No,” Valentine answered in an honest voice. “But no matter to him. If my sons do not bring this money within the seven days, they are dead. *Morti*. You understand?” Valentine focused back on the peppermint fudge. “You help me locate this killer, this person who poison Joseph Stally. If we find him...I will pay...I will pay the money he wants.” The man did not look at her, as if he did not even question whether she would help him or not; he simply assumed she would.

Rhonda shook her head. “Mr. DeVivo, my sister and I are retired, law-abiding citizens. We can't...and won't...break the law for anyone. If your sons are being threatened, you need to report--”

“Report? Report my sons? My own family? To the feds?” Valentine asked Rhonda, his thick gray eyebrows rising into his wrinkled forehead in shock and anger. “In this family, it is not done. You learn to trust no one. I do what has to be done to make sure business runs smooth.”

Valentine glanced at Rita and then back to Rhonda. "Smooth. Understand? No feds. I will pay this man who killed Joey, to spare my sons. That is not breaking the law. That is a father caring for his sons. *Nu padri, capisciu*?"

"Mr. DeVivo, if I find out who killed Joey Stally, he will be arrested," Rhonda promised. "I'm going to abide by the law." Rhonda steadied herself. "I'm not sure what you were expecting to find, Mr. DeVivo, but you're asking the wrong person for help."

Valentine slowly removed the sunglasses from his face and locked eyes with Rhonda. "You and your sister are why my Vincenzo, my Vinnie, is in jail today. As for Franco… Frank did something very stupid and got put in prison himself. But Vinnie--"

"Vinnie DeVivo murdered Chuck Langston."

"Langston was no-good rat," Valentine snapped in a hard voice. In the background, Rhonda spied Rita tense up and begin to go for her gun. Rhonda subtly shook her head no. "My son rid the world of a rat and nothing more."

"Your son murdered a man and is paying the penalty."

Valentine narrowed his eyes. "Ms. Knight, I am truly sorry for the monster I once was," he said in a low whisper, "but if anything happens to my two sons, you are to blame for not listening when I came to you and asked for help. And then I am not responsible if sleeping monsters wake up and find you and your sister here in sweet little village in the hills."

"Don't threaten me, Mr. DeVivo," Rhonda warned Valentine.

Valentine slowly put the sunglasses back over his eyes. "I am a man who never threatens," he said. "I am a man who makes good on my word."

"I'm not going to help you, Mr. DeVivo," Rhonda said, holding her ground.

"If you cannot help me," Valentine replied, "say goodbye to nice home, nice bakery, and nice sister, because rest of my life I will dedicate to your suffering." Before Rhonda could respond to this final, outrageous threat, Valentine simply turned and walked away with no concern.

Rita hurried up to Rhonda. "We have a fight on our hands," she said in a worried voice. "A man like Valentine DeVivo never goes back on a threat."

"Tell me about it," Rhonda said in a miserable voice, watching Valentine walk down an autumn leaf-covered sidewalk. "That man has really put the cherry on top of this awful day."

"Surely it can't get any worse," Rita said and walked Rhonda back to their SUV.

Brad leaned back against an old 1978 Westinghouse stove, took out his wooden pipe, lit it, and said: "I could arrest Mr. DeVivo."

“I'm sure Valentine DeVivo has a team of lawyers who will eat us alive if we arrest him on charges of threats,” Rhonda told Brad as she worked on getting a bottle of cold water down. The bakery felt warm after they had spent some time moving the heavy old appliances toward the back door and they still had a ways to go. “Besides, can we even prove what he said, Rita?”

Rita nodded. “Not really,” she said and went back to munching on the candy bar in her hand. Whenever Rita was upset she turned to junk food. Unlike Rhonda, who had the discipline to eat bran muffins for breakfast, Rita craved chocolate but seldom gave in to her desires until her nerves demanded otherwise. Sugar was Rita's hidden friend that helped her remain calm under pressure. “Besides, I don’t think his threats are the real problem. Mr. DeVivo isn't a stupid person, Brad. He's concerned about the welfare of his two sons, awful creatures that they are, and he will do anything to save them. He’s more valuable to us walking around, where we can hopefully track him, than he is in a holding cell, where a lawyer will spring him out, and then he’ll go underground. It’ll be useless getting any info out of him then.”

“Plus he’s too smart. His threats won't hold up in a court of law,” Rhonda finished for her sister. “He’ll unleash sleeping monsters? That could mean anything. There’s nothing substantial. Hey, that candy bar looks good.”

“Have it,” Rita offered. “I have another in my purse.”

"Uh..." Rhonda paused, darted her eyes over at Brad, and then shook her head no. "You know I have my reasons for wanting to stay healthy."

"I know," Rita sighed and polished off her candy bar. "But when times are tough my stress can only pay attention to the present situation, what can I say?" Rita looked down at her stomach. "I'm very thankful we come from parents who stayed skinny no matter what they ate. I never met a dish of ice cream I couldn't walk off in an hour."

From across the room, puffing on his pipe, Brad looked at Rhonda and then Rita. He wondered why the two women—two women who were very beautiful in body and heart—and neither were married. Surely, Brad thought, the two had caught the eyes of many men, men who were obviously too stupid to understand the sweet love each had to offer. But Brad knew it was better to not ask than to ask and offend, and risk upsetting delicate subjects. Sure, Rita and Rhonda were tough on the outside, but Brad knew, like most, likely had delicate hearts that needed love and not prying questions. "Doctors call that having high metabolism," he told Rita. "Some folks are blessed that way."

"I guess so," Rhonda told Brad and glanced down at her stomach with eyes that wondered why bran muffins were so important. "Stay healthy...find love," she whispered.

"What?" Brad asked.

"Oh, nothing," Rhonda told Brad. "Just an old, silly saying I always tell myself." Rhonda put down her water and looked around the kitchen. “Okay, back to the case before we move these hunks of junk out the door,” she said.

“We know that Vinnie and Frank DeVivo are being threatened because someone believes they know where Joey hid the money he stole.”

“Money he didn't turn over to the feds,” Rhonda added.

Rita nodded. “Valentine DeVivo thinks we can lead him to the killer…”

“…In order to pay the killer the money being demanded and to spare the lives of his two sons,” Rhonda finished for her sister. Brad was impressed how the two women worked together like a well-oiled machine. Of course, he thought, twins are always in tune with one another and understood what the other was thinking. “What we don't have are any leads to follow, never mind clues about how Joey figured out to come to Clovedale Falls, assuming the killer didn’t just dump him here.”

“And why the killer left Joey's body in the candle shop?” Rita added.

“But we do suspect that the killer is still in Clovedale Falls,” Rhonda told Brad.

“But we don't think that the killer will try and harm us,” Rita continued.

“Why do you think that?” Brad asked and began puffing on his pipe.

Rita debated on the second candy bar resting in her purse but then decided against it. “Rhonda and I believe that if the killer wanted us dead--”

“We would be dead this very second,” Rhonda told Brad. “The killer is looking for something else, not just blood. Must be the money. Also,” she continued, “Joey was killed in a non-violent manner. The killer stuck a syringe full of poison in Joey's neck.”

“Lewis Stevens isn't known to be clean when he kills somebody, by the way,” Rita told Brad. “And Valentine DeVivo and his sons...well, they are very cruel.”

“Which leads us to believe that the killer is connected to someone who wants to keep his business nice and clean,” Rhonda explained.

Brad puffed on his pipe for a minute and let Rita and Rhonda's words roam around his mind. “The feds?” he finally asked.

Rita was taken aback at this suggestion, but she didn’t want to rule out a crooked federal agent, either. “Either the feds or someone connected to the prison Vinnie and Frank are rotting in,” Rita nodded.

“Joey was killed before he could talk to us,” Rhonda went on. “Our theory is that Joey was in front of the bakery, waiting for us to arrive, and the killer got to him.”

“That makes sense,” Brad agreed.

“And we have one other theory,” Rita added, “which is wild in itself, but could explain why Joey's body was left in the candle shop.” Rita looked at her sister. Rhonda nodded. “We called Erma and asked her a few questions about Lilly DeLoach. We inquired about her personal life, her history, her family, and her candle shop.”

“Lilly DeLoach came up clean as a whistle, as we assumed she would,” Rhonda said.

“But,” Rita added, “Erma did tell give us one tidbit of information that we found very interesting.”

“What was that?” Brad asked, genuinely befuddled. He thought he knew everything of note about the little village’s inhabitants, and it seemed odd that Mrs. DeLoach would be involved in any way, as sweet as she was.

“Lilly is a very forgetful woman who, according to Erma, is always losing or misplacing things,” Rita told Brad. “She also frequently forgets to lock up behind herself.”

“Erma informed us that Lilly has lost the keys to her house, car, and candle shop on many occasions,” Rhonda added.

“Erma told us she even keeps a spare key to Lilly's house and her store, just in case,” Rita told Brad.

“You two ladies are wondering if Lilly left the front door to her shop unlocked?” Brad asked.

“Or left the keys to the front door hanging in the lock,” Rita nodded.

"And Joey Stally, while waiting for us to arrive at the bakery, could have seen the keys...or found the front door to the candle shop unlocked...and sneaked inside to hide himself," Rhonda said. "But of course, this is only a theory."

"I didn't find any signs of a forced entry," Brad pointed out and took a puff from his pipe. "The candle shop showed no signs of a struggle, either. The place was neat and clean. Nothing appeared to have been touched or tampered with."

Rita thought about the second candy bar again and then looked at Brad. "If our theory is correct," she said in a careful voice, "why would the killer leave Joey's body out in the open? That's the one question we don't have an answer to."

"Rita and I believe it's possible the killer left Joey's body out as a message," Rhonda said, anxious to start renovating the kitchen. She fiddled with the old cupboard nearest to her, straightening the door on its hinges. "But assumptions are meant to be nibbled on and not gobbled down. We don't want to arrive at a conclusion until we have concrete facts to stand on."

Rita studied Brad's eyes. "Okay, we spilled the beans on our end. What did you find out?"

Brad worked on his pipe for a few seconds and then lowered it from his mouth. "Warden Hank Miller is a clean man," he said. "Warden Miller has been married for forty-two years, served twenty-two of those years in the Air Force, has three children, two sons and daughter, a

Master's Degree in criminal justice, and a whole bunch of other stuff that puts the man on a pedestal."

"How long has this man been Warden at the prison?" Rita asked.

"Five years," Brad explained. "He replaced a man named Ryan Purdue. Ryan Purdue is currently serving a long prison term for corruption and dereliction of duty as a warden." Brad studied his pipe. "The Governor wanted a clean man to take over in order to please the public after Purdue's case got so much negative press. Someone squeaky clean and good for public relations. Hank Miller was just the right person. Since he has taken over, new work programs have been developed, substance abuse and alcohol workshops implemented, GED classes offered, and chaplains allowed back inside the prison walls. Hank Miller has designed a Work and Trust program in cooperation with Georgia that allows inmates with minor convictions to leave the facility and work in the community. All in all, ladies, the man has turned a very deadly and corrupt prison into a functioning rehabilitation center."

"What about the inmates on death row?" Rhonda inquired.

Brad tapped his pipe against a wooden counter and put it back into his right pocket. "Currently there are seven inmates on death row. Warden Miller has made it clear that the inmates on death row and those serving life in prison for murder will not receive the same treatment as the inmates who are in for, say, small-time drug convictions, petty larceny, stuff that gets you a few years or less."

"Which means Vinnie and Frank aren't out on work release or inside getting pedicures," Rhonda said.

"Those two rats are serving life in prison," Brad nodded his head. "Now, if I was a gambling man, I'd say they're scheming a way to escape from the prison. I know I would be."

"Say, that's right," Rhonda said in a curious voice. "A new warden might be making it extra hard on them, too. Perhaps it is their motivation for getting out now – no more corrupt warden to help them live a cushy life on the inside."

Rita rubbed her chin. "And who would help them?" she asked. "Why, dear old daddy of course."

"That's right," Rhonda agreed. "Valentine DeVivo isn't the type of criminal to sit back and let his two sons rot in prison." Rhonda lowered her eyes down to an old wooden floor marked with years of wonderful baking and began to think about Vinnie and Frank DeVivo, or Vincenzo and Franco as their father had called them. It was hard to square Valentine's loving, protective demeanor with his deadly threats of violence. "There's a lot of paths we could walk down right now, Rita."

"Too many," Rita agreed.

"So let's work this out," Rhonda said. "I'll focus on Vinnie and Frank and you focus on Joey and we'll meet in the middle. Deal?"

"Deal," Rita agreed and looked at Brad. "I need to talk to the agent who was in charge of Joey Stally."

"I can make a phone call," Brad said, feeling a hint of the old days ignite inside of his gut. Real cops doing real, honest police work felt great; just like back then when he was at the top of his game.

"Please," Rita told Brad. "If the feds are behind Joey's killing, I need to find out."

"And I'll investigate the prison," Rhonda explained. "Maybe this Warden Miller isn't as clean as he appears. Maybe Vinnie and Frank made a deal with him in exchange for their freedom. Maybe," Rhonda pondered, "Warden Miller is the man Valentine DeVivo is trying to pay off?"

"Joey is our main lead," Rita said in a careful voice. "He'll lead us to the killer."

Brad nodded his head. "Alright, ladies, we have work to do. Let's get to it."

"First," Rhonda said in a quick voice, "we need to come to an agreement."

"An agreement?" Brad asked.

Rhonda nodded. "Brad, my sister and I have tangled with some pretty bad alley cats in our day. But those days are over. We're beginning fresh new lives right here in Clovedale Falls."

Rita read her sister's eyes. “What Rhonda is trying to say is that we don't want to become known as...cops again,” she explained. “Rhonda and I want to be seen as two women who own a wonderful bakery. Does that make any sense to you?”

Brad nodded his head. “What you're trying to say is that you don't want me turning you two ladies into superheroes in the eyes of the town.”

Rhonda acknowledged acceptance. “We'll work on this case but stand in the shadows doing it. I know that might not be what you prefer, but we have our future to think about. The last thing we want or need is to turn our bakery into a pit stop for lazy cops and cheesy police talk and gossip--”

“That's laying it on pretty thick,” Brad objected. “My guys are good men.”

“Oh, I’m letting my mouth run. I guess I just mean, I need there to be separation between what we do as cops and what we do as bakers,” Rhonda said. “You understand what I'm saying?”

“My sister and I are worried that if the people of Clovedale Falls sees us as cops and not two women who own a bakery, well, they might shy away from us,” Rita told Brad. “The public has a tendency to shy away from cops...cops have a tendency to stick with cops.”

Brad put a gentle smile on his face. “Ladies,” he said in a caring, honest voice, “the folks who live in Clovedale Falls still respect the law because we have earned their respect.”

Brad looked deeply into Rita and Rhonda's eyes. "You two ladies will be accepted, or rejected, in Clovedale Falls for who you are, not for the nametag on your shirt. Folks look at the heart of people, and that's what makes them special. Don't matter if you're a cop or a librarian or a doctor. I know how folks are in the big cities and how cops are treated...I know there are a lot of rotten cops out there causing a bad name for us, and that's causing folks to put up a barrier. But it's not that way here."

Rita and Rhonda glanced at each other and realized that they had a lot to learn about Clovedale Falls. "The outside world has really scarred us, hasn't it?" Rhonda asked Rita.

"I suppose it has," Rita sighed. "Here we are wanting to be accepted and trusted, but we're the ones not accepting or trusting."

"Give it time," Brad told Rita. "You ladies have begun a new chapter in your lives in a strange new town. It's going to take time to find your sea legs. Don't expect it to happen overnight."

"I guess not. That's very good advice," Rita said and smiled at Brad. She checked the clock and straightened up, all business. "We better make our phone calls."

"Let's save the appliance moving for later. I'll call Roger," Rhonda told Rita. "I know he's busy but I'm sure if I bend his ear long enough I can get him to investigate Warden Miller for me."

"Deal," Rita said and looked around the kitchen. The kitchen was full of sweet whispers from the past; whispers filled with the scent of decent living. Rita craved to become part of those whispers. But first she had a job to do and a murder to solve.

Outside the bakery, Valentine DeVivo strolled by with a sour expression on his face, his powerful hands clasped behind his back.

5

Erma carried an old fashioned soup tureen patterned with yellow and red leaves into the coziest dining room Rita and Rhonda had ever seen. “Hot,” Erma said holding the pot with two white oven mitts. She carefully set the pot down onto a wooden pot holder on a square dining room table set for a queen. But the fancy table, although amazing to look at, wasn't what appealed to Rita and Rhonda. The two sisters were caught up in the atmosphere of the whole home: its autumn-hued walls, the soft carpets, the smell of cinnamon and pumpkin spice dancing in the air, and most importantly, all the special touches of a woman who loved her home.

“Smells great,” Rita smiled at Erma, admiring the graceful brown and white dress the woman had changed into after preparing a delicious supper.

Rhonda agreed as she sat down across from Rita and slowly spread a brown and red napkin across her lap.

"Erma, you really shouldn't have gone to so much trouble," she said, spotting a plate full of fresh, homemade, mouthwatering biscuits.

Erma smiled. "In my home, sweetie, the people I care about eat very well. Now, let me go get the sweet tea." Erma hurried off through a door that led into the kitchen that made Rita and Rhonda feel like they were in Aunt Bee's house in legendary Mayberry.

"I have to admit," Rhonda whispered as her eyes absorbed the sight of the delicious foods on the table, "after the day we had, I don't mind sitting down to a warm, home-cooked meal."

Rita softly tapped an autumn tablecloth patterned with pumpkins and leaves. "Erma said she made this tablecloth herself," she whispered back. "All that's left is for Andy and Barney to come walking through the door."

Rhonda looked down at the floor and saw an orange tabby cat rubbing itself against the leg of her chair. "Well, this guy isn't Andy," she said picking up the cat, "but he sure is a cutie."

Rita watched her sister pet the cat for a few seconds and then carefully set him back down on the floor. "Let's agree to not think about the day we had until we return home," she told Rhonda. "Right now my mind is completely exhausted. All I want to do is enjoy a warm meal with a new friend."

"Agreed," Rhonda said and quickly patted her lower left ankle. "I'm prepared just in case."

Rita sighed. “Me too, I'm afraid,” she whispered. “I never thought I would wear my gun in an ankle holster ever again. The tragedy of it all is that my gun feels natural up against my ankle.”

“I know what you mean,” Rhonda whispered back. “It's like Brad said...we're not going to learn to walk in Clovedale Falls overnight and we're not going to stop feeling like cops just because a piece of paper states that. It's going to take time, Rita...lots of time. But hey, you know what, we have time.”

“I'll feel a lot better about having all the time I need to readjust to life as a civilian after we close out this case. I didn't get nowhere with that crabby agent I spoke to today. The guy was tight lipped and rude. All that jerk did was reiterate what he told Brad: Joey went missing two weeks ago.”

“I know what you mean,” Rhonda mumbled. “I couldn't even get Roger on the phone. When I decided to call the prison myself and try to speak with Warden Miller, I hit a brick wall. I was told Warden Miller wasn't taking phone calls and to leave him a message on his voicemail.”

“Warden Miller is in charge of a very large prison,” Rita pointed out.

“I know,” Rhonda replied. “I struggled not to jump to any conclusions and reminded myself that being a prison warden is very demanding. But Rita, I kept having the feeling that the guy wasn't even at the prison. The woman I spoke to made it seem like he was on the prison grounds, but..." Rhonda quickly stopped herself. "Hey, didn't we just agree to not talk about our day until we got home? And look at me...babbling away like a woman with her mouth caught in a blender."

Rita rolled her eyes. "A woman caught with her mouth in a blender would be going to the hospital."

"Oh," Rhonda pouted, "you laugh at your dry British comedies and surely you understand when I'm joking."

"British comedy is relaxing and controlled," Rita pointed out and placed a napkin down onto her lap in a dignified manner.

Rhonda felt a grin touch her lips. "Sister of mine...Mr. Bean isn't relaxing or controlled. Mr. Bean is a nut! So there."

Rita frowned. She didn't like it when Rhonda made fun of her television shows.

"The only thing funny about that show is the book Lionel Hardcastle wrote about his life in Kenya. So there," Rhonda said and prepared for war.

Rita's face turned red. "Lionel Hardcastle is a very distinguished character.....you...silly twit."

"Silly twit?" Rhonda asked and then grabbed her chest as if Rita had stabbed her with a knife. "Oh, the pain...the agony...the suffering...someone call Fawlty Towers and get Basil. Of course poor Basil is probably too busy hiding a dead body."

"Oh, you make me so mad," Rita steamed good naturedly. "Why must you make fun of my British comedies? Do I make fun of the slapstick you watch? Do I?"

Rhonda grinned. "Rita, I make fun of the slapstick I watch. I mean, come on, that's the whole point! Besides, making fun of Laurel and Hardy on a rainy night with a bowl of popcorn is a blast. Sure beats being stood up on a blind date."

"Laurel and Hardy are two imbeciles who need to be locked away in a mental home," Rita rolled her eyes. "And don't get me started on I Love Lucy. That woman's show is enough to give me ulcers."

"Exactly," Rhonda laughed. "That's the fun of it. Remember the episode where Lucy and Ethel get a job at the chocolate factory?"

"Who doesn't, Rhonda? That episode is famous," Rita sighed. "I personally thought it was nerve-wracking."

"Bingo," Rhonda laughed again. "Comedy...clean and fun, not that awful trash they show today...it's supposed to be like an old friend you can visit anytime you want. A friend that will make you laugh, make you feel like you want to have a nervous breakdown, make you feel silly...all kinds of fun, different emotions."

"I prefer my British comedies over...Lucy Ricardo and Ethel Mertz. However," Rita admitted against her will, "I did like Ricky Ricardo's character."

"That's because you liked his accent," Rhonda teased.

"I did not," Rita fussed. "The man is dead, for crying out loud. Show some respect."

"Desi Arnaz died on December 2, 1986, Rita. But his character lives on in your heart, I can tell! Anyway, I'm sure the guy would still like people laughing at his show," Rhonda told Rita and offered a warm smile. "It's nice when a person leaves behind something that can still make people smile. Dad...bless his heart, he's a good man, but he's about as funny as a rock in a desert."

"Dad is a very practical person and I respect that."

"Yeah, he is," Rhonda agreed. "Mom sure has a funny bone, doesn't she. I always knew I got my funny side from her and you got your...practical side...from Dad. But that's what makes life great. Not everybody has a funny bone and not everybody can be serious all the time."

"Now isn't the time to be funny," Rita reminded Rhonda. "We're no further right now than we were this morning. We don't know who killed Joey. Sure, Valentine DeVivo opened up a few ideas for us, but that's all."

Before Rhonda could reply, Erma walked back into the dining room carrying a glass pitcher of sweet iced tea. "Now," she said in a motherly happy voice, "I have the pumpkin pie cooling. I decided to go with pumpkin pie instead of my usual pound cake. I hope you girls don't mind."

"Not at all," Rhonda promised in a happy voice. "Rita and I love pumpkin pie."

"We sure do," Rita smiled and watched Erma sit down at the head of the table. "Supper looks amazing, Erma. We're very happy you invited us."

"I hope this is the first of many suppers together," Erma smiled at Rita and then reached out her hands. "Let's give thanks to the Lord for this food."

Rita and Rhonda took Erma's hand, bowed their heads, and listened to Erma say the sweetest prayer they had ever heard. "Amen."

"Amen," Erma smiled and carefully filled three clear glasses. "The soup is still hot. While it's cooling I thought we could sit for a minute and talk."

"That sounds nice," Rhonda told Erma and took a sip of her tea. It nearly melted in her mouth. "That's delicious."

Rita hurried and took a drink of hers. "My, that is good," she complimented Erma.

"Years of practice," Erma blushed. "My momma taught me how to make sweet tea the right way." Erma smiled as her eyes misted over with warm memories. "In the old days, when times were really good, people understood how to live. Oh sure, my folks lived through the Great Depression but they found ways to be happy and came out stronger people for it, in the end. My folks understood what living was all about and never let life's little bumps get in the way."

"I can't imagine living during that time," Rhonda sighed. "The days when women still wore dresses, took evening walks with their beaus, picked blackberries together, held hands under the stars..."

Erma saw sadness enter Rhonda's sweet eyes. "Honey, forgive me for asking, but why aren't you married? You're a beautiful woman and so is your sister. Why, you two should have men lined up around the block begging to take you out for supper."

"Mr. Right is a very shy fella," Rhonda tried to joke but failed, the smile dying on her lips. "The right man just hasn't showed up yet, I'm afraid."

Rita took another drink. "My sister and I have dated...on and off...over the years," she told Erma as the sound of heavy rain began to fill the dining room. "I guess Mr. Northfield was right. It's raining."

"Chester must have been mighty grumpy today," Erma smiled and patted Rita's hand. "Continue, my dear."

"Oh, there's not much to tell," Rita blushed a little.

"What about that banker?" Rhonda asked. "You two were very close for a while. He even proposed to you."

"Sure," Rita sighed, "and then I caught him stealing money out of my purse."

Rhonda winced. "Oh yeah, forgot about that. Sorry."

"Working on the police force took up a lot of our time," she (Rita) explained to Erma. "It was always hard to find time to go on a date or take a day off. Atlanta is a lot different than Clovedale Falls. There's a lot of crime and a lot of demand for overtime."

"And our lives really got busy when Rita and I became detectives," Rhonda told Erma. "Tracking down killers take up a great deal of your time. It's not like the movies or television where the good guy catches the killer in one day."

"I bet," Erma said.

"Our first case," Rita said and then paused. "Oh, you wouldn't be interested."

"Yes, I would," Erma promised. "Honey, I live alone and it's seldom I have company. You wouldn't know, but folks like to stay home at night and rest, the same as I do. Oh, I have company over sometimes...mostly Lilly...but most of the time I eat supper alone with my cat, watching the old games shows I recorded over the years on my VCR. I'm glad for the company and even more glad to hear your stories. Go on now, tell me."

"Well...if you're sure," Rita said.

"I would be honored," Erma beamed.

Rita smiled at Erma's warm honesty. "Okay," she said and put down her tea. "Rhonda and I were assigned to our very first case. We were both very excited...and a little uncertain."

"A man had been found dead in the backyard of a pretty rough neighborhood," Rhonda jumped in. "A small-time drug dealer that had been shot down. Nothing major...but a murder nonetheless."

"My goodness," Erma said.

"Rookie detectives always get the small-time stuff at first," Rita explained. "Rhonda and I needed to get our feet wet and prove that we could handle a small case."

"Did you?" Erma asked.

"We sure did," Rhonda said in a proud voice. "Rita and I tracked down a twenty-year-old drug addict hiding out his aunt's basement."

"Not immediately, though," Rita pointed out. "After two weeks of asking questions, reviewing evidence, and going over the crime scene again and again, we managed to narrow down a list of suspects and began tracking them down."

"One night...it was raining as I recall...we spotted our killer sneaking into his aunt's home," Rhonda told Erma. "Rita and I had been following the aunt all day."

"Why?" Erma asked.

"A few people we talked to claimed the aunt was transporting drugs out of her house," Rita explained. "We put two and two together, staked out the house, and spotted her nephew--"

"Who matched the description of the killer that a small child gave the police," Rhonda quickly added.

Rita nodded. “And that's how we solved our first case. No flashy lights and red carpet...just basic police work.”

“Which takes a lot of time,” Rhonda pointed out. “Try getting a date when you're parked in an unmarked police car all night eating Chinese food...doesn't happen.”

“I suppose it wouldn't,” Erma agreed. She reached over and patted Rhonda's hand. “The good Lord has His reasons, honey. The right man will come along at the right time, I promise.”

“I hope the right man comes along before I'm too old to remember his name,” Rhonda joked and patted her stomach. “If I eat one more dry bran muffin I'm going to turn into a husk of a woman and crumble into millions of little pieces.”

Erma laughed. “Well, let's hope my pumpkin pie will satisfy your appetite. And speaking of appetite,” Erma turned to Rita, “I have decided to give you girls all of my old recipes.”

“Recipes?” Rita asked.

“Recipes to every goody I have ever baked over the years,” Erma beamed. “All the town favorites, everything that won the bake-offs, special occasion cakes, you name it.” She paused, looking bashful. “Now, you girls don't have to--”

“We'll take them!” Rhonda exclaimed and smiled happily at Rita. “What do you know,” she said, “there is a happy ending to this day after all.”

Then the telephone rang, and the sisters both knew that sound was going to bring unexpected news. They just didn't know what kind, and would have to wait to find out.

Billy watched Rita turn her SUV down a bumpy dirt road saturated with heavy rain. The dirt road splintered off into smaller lanes that traveled through acres and acres of farmland, apple orchards, corn fields, and pumpkin patches. Billy knew each lane by heart, but he was the only one. It was better, he figured, to meet the law at the front of the dirt road that ran in front of his two-story farmhouse instead of trying to explain where he had found the dead body. "What a night," he said, feeling a bit silly wearing his oversized green poncho over his coveralls. Billy didn't mind the poncho or the rain. What he did mind was the poncho's great big hole in the hood, and thus his favorite hat getting all wet. But that was life.

"There's Billy," Rhonda told Rita and pointed at a man standing next to an old tractor hooked to a wooden wagon with a roof, a covered hayride without the fun, sitting in the dark as it was.

"I don't see Brad's car," Rita commented as she eased her SUV over one muddy rut after another. "My goodness, how do people live like this."

"I'm sure this road is like I-75 to Billy," Rhonda told Rita, watching the windshield wipers fight rain off. "Billy is a farmer. He's tough and used to working the land, even when the mud's up to his knees. Us city folks are soft and expecting smooth roads leading to fancy coffee shops."

"I suppose," Rita agreed as her vehicle crawled up to Billy.

Rhonda quickly rolled down the window and popped her head out. "Hello, Billy," she called out through the rain.

Billy walked up to the SUV and put his right hand over his eyes. "I wasn't sure you would find my place," he said and offered Rita a polite hello. "Sheriff ain't here yet. Best that we should wait for him."

Rita leaned her head over her sister and looked at Billy. "Where is the body, Billy?" she asked.

"Way down in the lower apple orchards," Billy explained. He pointed into the dark (delete), (it is dark at night) night. "Southeast of my house a ways. I got the roofed wagon attached to the tractor so we can haul it out. I don't reckon the county coroner has any equipment capable of getting in and out of the fields in this mud. Won't take no more than about twenty minutes to get to where we need to be."

"Twenty minutes?" Rita asked.

"I own a lot of land," Billy explained. "Take you from sunrise to lunch time just to walk half my land."

"Goodness," Rhonda exclaimed. "How do you take care of so much land?"

"Nature does a lot of the work," Billy explained. "Most of my land is farmed...apple trees...corn fields...pumpkin patches...cider houses….work buildings...barns next to the hay fields...and even got myself a whole bunch of cows grazing in the far north pasture. I only mow the yard around my house and keep the main lanes trimmed down that folks use during the festival."

Rhonda closed her eyes, listened to the rain, and for a few seconds imagined growing up on a huge farm. She saw herself feeding chickens, planting seeds, picking corn, milking cows, and making homemade apple butter. Then she saw herself sitting in a run-down gray pickup in a dirty parking lot attached to a closed-down carpet factory. Farm work was hard and there wasn't a whole lot of industry out in these rural areas. "You're very blessed, Billy," she said, looking around. "You're living a real nice life."

"A hard life," Billy pointed out. "Running this farm is mighty hard work. I wake up an hour before the sun wakes up and go to bed an hour after the sun tells me goodnight. And that's only during the spring and summer months. When it turns autumn and the festival starts getting close I get maybe six hours' sleep a night." Billy looked into the rainy night. "Reckon I won't get much sleep tonight," he said and shook his head. "Never had a dead body on my land before. Jose nearly wet his pants when he stumbled across the body."

Rita focused on Billy. "Billy, can you tell us what the dead man looks like again?" she asked.

"Reckon I can," Billy told Rita. "Old fella wearing a black rain coat," he continued. "Fancy suit under that, real shiny shoes, you know, city shoes. He had thick gray hair." Billy was describing Valentine DeVivo in perfect detail, which made both Rita and Rhonda's stomachs drop with uneasiness. “I reckon I might have done wrong but I checked his pockets, hoping to find a wallet...to see who he was, you know. I didn't find nothing.”

“You didn't do wrong, Billy,” Rhonda assured Billy.

Billy shoved his hands into the front pockets of his poncho. “Two dead fellas in one day,” he said and shook his head. “Sheriff is going to have to cancel the festival for sure.”

“Sheriff Bluestone has assured us that there's too much business on the line, so he's not going to cancel the festival,” Rita told Billy and offered him a supportive smile. She liked Billy and admired his simple ways—simple ways that in her view were a treasure in a world filled with hypocrites dressed up like intellectuals. Rita knew she would rather spend a year speaking with Billy about his pumpkins than spend a single minute speaking with some snobby scholar about ethical philosophical or whatever. Billy came about his knowledge honestly, from the land. There was not a pretentious bone in his body. Billy was an honest man who didn't hide who he was, and that, to Rita, made the man a real genius in her eyes.

“I don't see how the sheriff can't cancel the festival,” Billy told Rita. “Two dead fellas means a lot of trouble for a little town like Clovedale Falls. Folks sure ain't gonna be lining up to come here this year when word gets out.” Billy looked down at his wet boots. “A lot of good folks are gonna take a hard financial nose dive this year, that's for sure.”

“Billy,” Rhonda said in a strong voice, “Sheriff Bluestone isn't going to cancel the festival.”

Billy raised his eyes. “I wish I could be sure.”

“You can be,” Rhonda promised. “There's more to this case than you understand right now,” she continued. “If the sheriff truly believed—or if my sister and I truly believed—the public was in any danger, we would cancel the festival. As it stands, we believe the killings are connected to an outside source and are directed to a threat that has nothing to do with the town itself. It’s just the outside world intruding on this little town and we don’t need to let it ruin everything.”

“I...whatever that means, I reckon I can accept it,” Billy said and then quickly pointed his left finger down the dirt road. “I spot some headlights coming our way. Must be the sheriff.”

Rita and Rhonda looked over their shoulders, spotted the headlights, and carefully pulled their guns free from their ankle holsters. “If it's not the Sheriff…” Rita said.

Rhonda nodded grimly, “…we shoot,” she finished. “But who else would be driving out here in this rain?” When asked, Billy confirmed that none of his workers were scheduled to come out along this road, so it couldn’t be anyone from the farm.

Rita drew in a deep breath. “Our safety comes first.”

“I know,” Rhonda agreed and waited for the approaching vehicle to reach the SUV. When she saw Brad climb out of the brown Sheriff's truck she quickly holstered her gun, grabbed a gray umbrella from the back seat, and stepped out into the rain. “Hello, Brad.”

“Glad you ladies could make it,” Brad told Rhonda, ignoring the heavy rain that was falling into the brown gray poncho he had slapped over his uniform.

“Remind me to get some plastic,” Billy told Brad.

“What?” Brad asked.

Billy pointed at the plastic bag Brad had wrapped around his sheriff's hat to protect it from the rain. “Oh,” Brad said and grinned briefly. “Gotta keep the brim dry.”

Rita put her gun away, reached into the back seat, grabbed a black umbrella, and made her way out to Brad, feeling like a lost woman entering a frozen scream of a nightmare. “Billy's description matches Valentine DeVivo,” she said in the calm voice she reserved for police work and then glanced around the dark land. In the daylight hours she would have seen apple trees, pumpkin patches, rows and rows of corn, and other autumn delights that would have warmed her heart. But the night was slick with mud and rain —perfect police weather. Police weather didn't permit warm and cozy feelings.

Billy tossed his thumb at the tractor. “I got the wagon ready. You guys go ahead and crawl in and I'll get us moving.”

“Thanks, Billy,” Brad said. “You ladies ready?”

"Ready," Rhonda told Brad and looked at Rita. "Are you ready?"

Rita searched the night with her eyes. "The killer could be watching us this very second, Rhonda. We could be sitting ducks."

Rhonda reached her eyes into the dark, wet landscape around them. "I know," she said in a miserable voice.

"No sense in standing out in this rain," Brad said. "We need to get to the body."

Rita nodded and carefully followed Rhonda to the back of the wagon. She spotted a wooden plank leading up to the wagon, smelled wet hay, and sighed. "My first hayride of the season...not the way I expected."

"Me, neither," Rhonda agreed. "Well, age before beauty."

"Thanks a lot," Rita complained and made her up way up the wooden plank and found a damp bale of hay to sit on. She tucked her umbrella in and looked around. "At least it's a little dry in here."

Rhonda hurried up into the wagon and plopped down next to Rita. "Next time remind me to wear tennis shoes. These heels are killing my feet," she said, folding her umbrella up.

"My feet are soaking wet," Rita said under her breath. "I'll be surprised if we don't catch pneumonia."

Brad made his way into the wagon, bent down, pulled the wooden plank up, and then yelled: “We're all set back here, Billy.”

Billy threw a thumbs up at Brad and climbed up into the tractor. “Here we go,” Rita said.

“Yes, here we go,” Rhonda agreed, hearing Billy bring the tractor to life.

Brad sat down on a bale of hay in front of Rita and Rhonda. “Any idea why Valentine DeVivo might have been killed?” he asked.

“Not yet,” Rita confessed.

Brad nodded his head, pulled out his pipe, lit it, and waited for Billy to get the tractor moving. A minute later the tractor started to slowly ease forward. “Billy is going to drive real careful,” he assured Rita and Rhonda. “Don't worry.”

Rita felt the tractor begin pulling the wagon forward. The wheels of the wagon began to whine and creak, rocking in the muddy ruts of the dirt road, but finally stopped resisting and gave way, rolling forward. “Whoever killed Valentine DeVivo is either a very brave man or a very stupid man,” she told Brad, drawing in a deep scent of wet hay.

“Valentine DeVivo's death won't go unanswered,” Rhonda added. “The man is still very powerful in Italy. His people will want answers.”

"I thought as much," Brad nodded his head and began working on his pipe.

Rita watched Brad puff on his pipe. The sight of the man and the smell of his pipe brought a strange comfort to her heart. "Brad, before we talk about Valentine DeVivo, we need to decide what we're going to do about the festival."

"I talked to the mayor," Brad explained. "The answer is still the same as earlier: the festival stays open. Too many folks in this town depend on the festival, ladies, including yourselves. I can't shut down the festival and let innocent people suffer."

Rhonda smelled the cherry tobacco wafting from Brad's pipe. The smell of the tobacco somehow dulled the sharp edge of the night. "We're glad the answer is still the same," she told Brad. "Rita and I were worried you might have changed your mind."

"We know it might seem counterintuitive, but we just don't feel that this case is a public threat," Rita explained as the back wheels of the wagon hit a deep mud puddle. Rita grabbed Rhonda and held on. When the wagon cleared the mud puddle she let go. "My, it is bumpy," she said.

Brad lowered his pipe. "The mayor wouldn't let me close the festival even if this case was a public threat," he pointed out. "If I tried, he would fire me and find a man who would ignore the threat. As it stands, I happen to agree with you ladies."

"We're glad,"Rhonda told Brad. "We're also hoping that we're right."

“The death of Valentine DeVivo is going to cause a war,” Rita said in a worried voice. “Benny DeVivo, Franks cousin, has taken over operations for the DeVivo Family in Atlanta. Rhonda and I don't know much about him because after Joey testified in court we were assigned to a new case.”

“But we do know that Benny, according to rumors at least, was pushing another family located in New Jersey pretty hard,” Rhonda told Brad. “But it's like my sister said. After Joey helped us put Vinnie DeVivo away we moved on to a new case.”

Brad took a puff from his pipe. “Are you girls suggesting that whoever killed Valentine DeVivo did so to start a mafia war?”

“A killer needs to cover his tracks,” Rhonda replied. “Starting a mafia war could be the perfect cover.”

“But before we jump to conclusions,” Rita said, remaining practical, “we need to make sure the dead man is Valentine DeVivo and then locate his driver.”

Brad looked into the darkness and found Rita and Rhonda's faces. Even though he could barely see them he felt their worry.

Rita and Rhonda sat very quietly for a few minutes. The seemingly small case was threatening to explode out of control. “We also need to find out who Warden Hank Miller really is,” Rhonda finally spoke. “My gut is telling me that man isn't so squeaky clean after all.”

"I agree," Rita nodded. "I know the agent I spoke to earlier gave us a hard time, but I don't believe the feds are involved. I think they're upset that Joey slipped through their fingers, but that's it. The agent who gave us a hard time earlier seemed to be protecting his pride rather than his innocence."

Brad considered Rita's words. "Okay," he said lowering his pipe, "we'll turn our full attention on Warden Miller and see what we can dig up. But you ladies know as well as I do that shaking the nest of high officials is going to cause us some backlash."

"We are used to taking backlash," Rita said in a steady voice. "That's part of the job. If the public isn't hating us it's one politician or another. The pursuit of justice has always come at a very severe price for those who are not willing to back down."

"In other words," Rhonda said, taking a deep breath of wet hay and cherry tobacco, "bring on the fight, because these two girls have a bakery to get in shape and don't have time to go twelve rounds. We're looking for a first round knockout."

Brad grinned. "I believe you are," he said in a proud voice. "I believe you two ladies just might get that knockout, too. Then again," he said, "we may all get knocked out. Time will tell."

"Time isn't on our side," Rita and Rhonda both said at the same time and then grew very silent as Billy pulled the wet wagon through the night.

6

Billy stopped the tractor on a wet, muddy lane snuggled in between rows of apple trees that seemed to stretch out forever like black bats fluttering in the night. Rita and Rhonda knew the black bats were just the leaves of apple trees fighting the wind, but their imaginations were working overtime and it was difficult to overcome the unwanted illusion. “Ready?” Brad asked.

Rita and Rhonda nodded their heads, stood up, and walked to the end of the wagon, and watched Brad set down the wooden plank. “Age before beauty,” Rhonda told Rita again.

“You're real funny,” Rita cracked. She pushed open her umbrella, (delete ,) and made her way down the wooden plank. The rain was falling much harder, making it difficult to see. “Rain, rain go away,” Rita whispered as Billy climbed off the tractor.

Rhonda popped open her umbrella, stepped out into the rain, and spotted Billy walking up to Rita. “How far, Billy?” she called out.

“Just over there,” Billy yelled over the rain and tossed his right thumb toward the left side of the lane.

Brad walked down the wooden plank, studied the night, and nodded his head toward Billy. “Let's go, Billy,” he said in a stern voice.

“Sure thing,” Billy replied and looked at Rita and Rhonda. He couldn't tell which sister was which. All he knew was that both women sure were pretty standing out in the rain. But he didn't have time to act like a silly school boy suffering from puppy love. A man was dead and Billy Northfield had a job to do. “This way,” he said somberly and trudged off into the rain.

“Let's go,” Rhonda whispered and started after Billy. Rita followed close behind. Brad Bluestone brought up the rear.

Billy quickly worked his way past one apple tree and then another, heading deeper into the orchard, stepping on fallen or rotten apples in shallow puddles of water, and then suddenly came to a stop. “There,” he called out, pointing down at the ground.

Rhonda rushed up to Billy, nearly tripping over the fallen apples lying on the ground, and looked to where he was pointing. She spotted a dark figure face down on the ground. “We have a body,” she called out to Rita and Brad.

Rita, nearly tripping over every apple she stepped on, hurried up to Rhonda, spotted the dead body, and nodded. "Billy," she said, "go back and secure the tractor. The killer could be anywhere."

"I have my rifle on the tractor," Billy promised. "Ain't no one gonna sneak off with it on my watch."

Brad stepped up beside Rita and spotted the dark, wet form of Valentine DeVivo. "Shoot first and ask questions later," he ordered Billy.

"I sure will," Billy promised and began to hurry away. But then he stopped, turned around, and looked at Rita and Rhonda. "My thinking is that whoever killed that fella ain't around," he said in a thoughtful voice. "Jose found that fella while he was taking a walk." Billy shook his head. "Maria had skipped out on supper with him again and Jose gets mighty sad when that happens and takes long walks through the orchards. Anyway, he found the body and made it back to me in one piece...and the body is still here, just the way I found it. Just saying."

Rita and Rhonda listened to Billy and then considered his words. "Billy is probably right," Rita admitted.

"Most likely," Rhonda agreed.

"You better get on back and guard the tractor just in case," Brad told Billy.

"You bet," Billy said and vanished into the rain.

"I'll check the body," Rhonda said. She walked over to Valentine DeVivo, bent down, and checked for a pulse. "No pulse...face feels cold...checking for gunshot wounds."

Rita watched her sister check the body, hoping that the killer wasn't doing the same. She felt vulnerable and open but knew being a cop meant putting your life on the line and dismissing personal safety. "Anything?" she asked.

"Nothing," Rhonda called back. "One thing is for sure, though, this man is definitely Valentine DeVivo." Rhonda stood up, brushed off her hands, and walked back to Rita and Brad. "My guess is that Mr. DeVivo was poisoned, just like Joey was."

"Doc Downing won't be here for a while. Mrs. Carrington's daughter went into labor about three hours ago," Brad explained. "Doc will be around after he delivers the baby."

"Oh, a baby," Rhonda sighed and softly touched her stomach. "I love babies."

"Me, too," Rita whispered to herself as she touched her own stomach. "More than you know."

Brad kept his eyes on the body. "Ladies, that fella was lured out to this apple orchard."

"Yes, that's our thinking," Rhonda agreed.

"Which means Valentine DeVivo was going to do business with the killer," Rita told Brad. "He surely didn't come way out here to talk about the weather with a stranger, nor would ever meet with a stranger to begin with. The man was dangerously smart, Brad."

"I'm wondering where his driver and car is," Rhonda asked. "Rita, you and I both heard Valentine tell his driver to get something to eat and return in one hour. That was this afternoon."

"I remember," Rita agreed. "I didn't see the driver, though. The windows on Valentine's car were too darkly tinted."

"I have my guys out on patrol looking for a car of the description you gave me," Brad informed them. "Maybe they'll catch someone on the loose tonight."

"Or maybe the driver ran out of town or is dead himself," Rita worried.

"Only time will tell," Brad replied. He reached into his front pocket, pulled out a black cell phone, ducked under Rita's umbrella, and made a call. "Anything?" he asked, putting the call on speaker phone.

"Town is sleepy, Sheriff," Deputy Phil Baker said, cruising down a quiet residential street lined with cozy two-story homes facing lawns covered with wet autumn leaves. "John ain't seen nothing, either. We've covered every inch of town. Matt and Steve are riding the county roads, but they're coming up empty handed, too."

"How is Doc Downing coming along?" Brad asked, searching the dark apple orchards with careful eyes.

“Stephanie Carrington just gave birth to a baby boy about twenty minutes ago,” Phil told Brad in a happy voice. “We have a new citizen in town.”

“Well, how about that,” Brad smiled.

“A baby boy,” Rhonda and Rita both sighed at the same time.

“A baby boy,” Brad smiled again and then focused his mind back on the case. “Okay, Phil, keep wasting gas until I get back to town.”

“You got it, Sheriff,” Phil promised and then added: “Sheriff, the dead man...is he really that mafia fella I read about?”

“Sure is,” Brad confirmed.

Phil whistled. “A dead mafia man right here in Clovedale Falls,” he said. “I've lived in this town my entire life and never saw such a thing before. About the only exciting thing that ever happened to me was watching Old Man McCuskey's barn burn down. Of course the old-timer was drunk on moonshine and knocked over his own oil lantern, just like Mrs. O’Leary’s cow in that old song...that crazy old coot.”

“Murder isn't exciting, Phil,” Brad pointed out.

“Oh, I know that's the truth,” Phil agreed. “I'm just saying that Clovedale Falls is going to be glowing with talk for years to come. Goodness, you better believe it.”

"Yeah, I guess you're right," Brad agreed. "I'll talk to you when I get back to town."

"You bet," Phil said and ended the call.

Brad shoved the cell phone back in his pocket. "Surprised I even got reception this far out," he said. "Still prefer the old radios, but the signal is no good out in these little pocket valleys and hills...never liked cell phones. Always feel like I'm betraying the old ways carrying this stupid thing around."

"Technology does help police work," Rita pointed out.

"I guess," Brad hesitantly agreed. "But I could have called Phil just as easily from Billy's house, too."

"Assuming Phil had a phone in his car," Rhonda said. "No way to call his radio from a phone, is there?"

Brad shrugged his shoulders. "Point taken," he conceded and looked around again. "We better get back to the tractor. Doc will be here soon. No sense in making him wait and--" Brad stopped talking when he saw a shadow move from one apple tree to another. "We're being watched," he whispered in a low, careful voice. "I saw--"

"We saw him," Rhonda whispered back, feeling the hairs stand up on the back of her neck.

Rita threw caution to the wind, slowly bent down, and retrieved her gun. Rhonda followed suit. Brad nodded his head and pulled out his own gun. "You there!" he called out, “behind the apple trees, come out this second or we're going to begin shooting!”

Rita and Rhonda backed up behind an apple tree and waited for bullets to begin flying. When silence prevailed instead of the sound of bullets erupting, they looked at each other. Brad eased behind an apple tree and knelt down. “You have to the count of ten,” he yelled.

“Why do I feel like I'm back in Atlanta preparing to storm a warehouse full of thugs?” Rhonda whispered, staring into the rain, searching for the shadow figure.

“I feel the same way,” Rita whispered, keeping her gun at the ready, feeling silly wearing high heels instead of reliable police shoes. “I just hope we don't have to go on a foot chase.”

“If we do, kick off your high heels and run barefoot,” Brad ordered.

“Running barefoot through a rainy apple orchard at night sounds squishy…but fun,” Rhonda sighed. “My reward will be a few twisted ankles, tree limbs slapping in the face, and maybe a dose of pneumonia.”

“All part of it,” Brad said, searching the rain. “Time is running out!” he yelled. “Show yourself right now or I begin shooting!”

Rita looked at Rhonda. “Let's make this real,” she said and fired two warning shots into the air. “You heard the sheriff,” she yelled into the air, “show yourself right now or we're coming after you!”

“Don't...shoot,” a man begged in a trembling voice. “It's me, Jose...I work for Billy Northfield…please...don't shoot.”

“Jose?” Brad asked and then yelled: “Jose, get out here!”

Jose Mendez eased out from behind an apple tree and slowly walked into a clearing with his hands raised high in the air. “Brad, I...” he began to speak but stopped, shaking.

Brad shook his head, put his gun away, and walked out to Jose. “What are you doing out here?” he asked in a softer tone.

Rita and Rhonda looked at each other, nodded their heads, and hurried out to the young man. Jose spotted Rita and Rhonda and tensed up even more than he already was. “Don't shoot me,” he begged Brad. “Tell them I work here. I didn’t do nothing.”

“Put your guns away, ladies,” Brad ordered. Rita and Rhonda did as ordered. “These two ladies are--”

“The two cops from Atlanta,” Jose told Brad, “I know.” He kept his hands raised high in the air as the heavy rain soaked his work clothes and a shock of wavy black hair that fell across his forehead. “Billy told me about them.”

“You can lower your arms,” Brad instructed Jose hesitated and then slowly lowered his arms. “Now, tell me Jose, what are you doing out in this apple orchard this time of night?”

Jose swallowed. He was a young man of twenty-two, thin as a reed, and more scared than a bird with a broken wing limping along the side of a busy road. “I...lied to Billy,” he said in a shaky voice.

“You lied?” Rhonda asked in a tough voice. With no mirrors around to see herself in, she felt capable of finally playing the bad cop without laughing at herself… “What do you mean you lied?”

Rita jumped into the act. “Cool down,” she told Rhonda, trying to play the good cop to her sister’s tough act. “Let the young man talk.”

“He better talk, because I want answers,” Rhonda demanded and pointed a hard finger at Jose. “Do you hear me?”

Brad fought back a grin. In her heels and half-soaked dress, Rhonda sounded as tough as a baby kitten defending its bowl of warm milk. The woman just didn't have a mean bone in her body. “Jose,” he said, “what exactly did you lie about?”

Jose stared at Rhonda through the rain. Maybe Brad didn't think she was mean, but he sure did. “I'm going to get in trouble,” he worried.

“No, you're not,” Brad asked. “Just tell me what happened.”

“My parents will send me back to Mexico to stay with my aunt,” Jose whined. “Maria will never speak to me again...” Jose looked down at the wet ground. “She's going to think I'm a coward...but I'm not, I swear. I lied because...I was afraid for my family...for Maria...for Mr. Billy. Billy has been good to me...a real friend. I came to his farm with my parents when I was five years old. Billy has practically raised me like his own. He taught me how to read and speak English after school, and how to drive a tractor and work the farm when I got old enough..." He sighed. "I don't want to see Billy hurt."

"Jose," Brad said and laid a gentle hand on the young man's shoulder, "if you care for Billy, tell us why you lied."

"Please," Rita asked Jose and softly moved her umbrella over his head, allowing the falling rain to wet her instead. "Please, speak to us. It could be the most important part of the case."

Jose raised his eyes, looked at Rhonda, and then begged her, tears in the corners of his eyes, "Please don't arrest me."

Rhonda caved in. She walked over to Jose and patted his shoulder. "I'm not going to arrest you, Jose. I was just playing the good-cop, bad-cop thing. Deep down I'm a softie," she promised. "Now, relax and talk to us, okay? No one is going to hurt you or arrest you. If you don't trust me, at least trust your friend the sheriff here. You're safe with us--" Rhonda stopped talking when she heard someone running toward their location. She spun around and saw Billy appear with his rifle.

"I heard shots!" Billy yelled out.

“It's okay, Billy,” Brad called out. “It’s Jose, we found him in the trees. Everything is under control.”

Billy hurried up to Brad, spotted Jose, and lowered his rifle. “Jose, what in the world are you doing out here?”

Jose looked at Billy with sorrowful eyes. “Billy,” he said and then broke out into tears. “Billy...I lied to you. I told you I found the body...the truth is...I saw the...I saw the murder happen.” Jose threw himself into Billy's arms. “I was scared for you, Billy...scared for all of us. Please don't send me away...please.”

Billy gently put his arms around Jose. “Now, now,” he said in the tone of a loving father, “Old Billy could never send you away. Why, you're like my own son.” He cradled the young man tenderly, bewildered by Jose’s tears.

Rita and Rhonda looked at each other and nodded their heads. They had just caught a break in the form of a very scared young man who happened to see a murder take place because his girl had refused to have supper with him. It’s strange how these things worked out sometimes, but it might prove to be exactly the break they needed.

Brad drove Jose back to town after Doc Downing hauled Valentine DeVivo's body away. Doc Downing had been very grumpy about being called out late at night, in the rain to retrieve a second body. Rita and Rhonda followed behind Brad, carrying one special passenger with them.

"We're glad you came along, Billy," Rhonda said with a smile, shaking rainwater out of her hair.

"Jose's folks are mighty scared and it wouldn't be fitting to leave the little fella alone in town," Billy explained, feeling like a sardine in a can. It wasn't that he minded riding in a nice SUV with two beautiful women, it was just that he was used to his old truck and the smell of Chester's dog hair. He felt a bit grubby and shabby in comparison to their nice clothes, and wished he presented a more gentlemanly figure. "Not a good night for my battery to go out on my truck, either," he said.

"Brad promised to drive you and Jose back to the farm," Rita told Billy and offered him a kind smile. "I'm kinda glad the battery went dead on your truck. Now we have time to talk."

"Talk?" Billy asked, feeling his cheeks turn red. What would two women like Rita and Rhonda want to talk to him about? He had already confessed all he knew about the dead body Jose had found.

"Billy," Rhonda asked in a casual tone of voice, "have you seen any strangers on your farm lately?"

"No ma'am," Billy promised, relaxing somewhat to hear an easy question. "I know all of my workers by face and name. Ain't no stranger been on my farm."

"Any idea why Valentine DeVivo's body was found on your farm?" Rita asked.

"Not a clue," Billy confessed.

“Aside from the obvious,” Rhonda added. “Joey's body was left in a candle shop and Valentine DeVivo's body was left in an apple orchard. The killer obviously wanted the bodies found.”

“Mafia war?” Rita asked. “More false clues meant to start the war?”

“What else could it be?” Rhonda answered. “I suppose there could be a few other possible explanations, but my gut is telling me we have a killer who wants to play a game.”

“What game?” Billy asked, taking in a deep scent of a pretty perfume. The inside of the SUV sure smelled...girly, he thought; it felt girly, too, with its plush, pristine upholstery and cute touches like a crystal something-or-other hanging down from the rearview mirror. Billy liked the smell of the perfume but wished he was riding in his old truck. A man needed his truck.

Rhonda turned around and found Billy looking toward the rearview mirror. The poor man looked like a prisoner trapped in a hole. “Are you okay?” she grinned.

“Oh...sure,” Billy said and gestured to the window. “Mind if I roll down the window and get a bit of fresh air?”

“Go right ahead,” Rita smiled.

Billy quickly let the window down a little, ignoring the rain, and drew in a deep breath of sweet night air. “That's better,” he said and turned his attention back to Rhonda. “What game?”

"Well," Rhonda explained, "say, for example, you wanted to kill a person who belonged to...say...a street gang."

"I ain't never wanted to kill nobody," Billy said uncomfortably. "No sir, the Bible teaches me to treat others as I want to be treated and to even love my enemies. Now, loving your enemies is sure hard to do, but Jesus sure loved me when I wasn't worthy."

Rhonda smiled. Billy's child-like insistence on his values was refreshing to the heart. "I'm only making an example," she promised. "I don't really want you to pretend you want to kill someone, of course."

"Oh...oh yeah, sure," Billy said and blushed a little. "I reckon I misunderstood you. Keep talking."

"Well," Rhonda continued, holding back a smile, "say you want to kill a person who belongs to a street gang, right?"

"I guess, okay."

"Now, you just can't kill someone in broad daylight, now can you?" Rhonda asked.

"Not unless you're mighty dumb."

"Exactly," Rhonda pointed out. "A person...a killer...will plan his murder first and create a backdoor to escape through. In this case, if the killer murdered a person belonging to a street gang, he might try to pin the murder on a rival gang in order to slip free. He might even try to pin it on a rival gang's other enemy, causing his two worst enemies to go to war with each other."

“While the killer gets away clean and easy,” Rita told Billy.

Billy rubbed his chin. “Folks really do that kind of thing?” he asked.

“Seen it happen a couple of times in Atlanta,” Rhonda sadly said and nodded. “Before Rita and I became detectives and were regular patrol cops, we worked some pretty rough neighborhoods and saw some pretty bad stuff go down.”

“We sure did,” Rita told Billy, carefully following the sheriff as they turned down another dark, rainy country road.

“What kind of stuff?” Billy dared to ask.

“We saw a drug dealer kill two gang members and blame it on another gang,” Rhonda explained. “The gang went to war over it. The same thing happened a couple of years later...same drug dealer, same method.”

“The drug dealer was eventually caught and he confessed,” Rita told Billy. “But not before the damage was done and a few kids were...lost...in the process.”

“Stupid kids trying to act tough.” Rhonda sighed.

“Stupid kids trying to act tough,” Rita agreed.

Rhonda shook her head. “Anyway, Billy, Valentine DeVivo runs the DeVivo Family. He's a big-time player who, even though he got kicked back to Italy, still managed to run his operation right here on American soil via his two sons."

"Valentine DeVivo also has a lot of enemies...people who want him dead," Rita explained.

Billy rubbed his chin again. "So what you girls are saying is that a lousy drug dealer just killed a street gang member and is going to try to pin the death on another gang. Except this is bigger than gangs, I reckon."

"Right," Rhonda told Billy. "Rita and I could be wrong, but because the bodies of both Joey and Valentine were left in open places, we're assuming this is the path the killer decided to take."

"You girls are mighty smart."

"Experienced," Rita pointed out. "We have twenty years of law enforcement experience, Billy. But even with all those years under our belt we're still just rookies."

"How do you figure?" Billy asked.

"Because each murder is new and each killer is different," Rhonda explained. "No matter how seasoned a cop is, if he or she walks into a murder case like a rooster with its chest stuck out, then that cop is going to fall flat on his or her face."

"A seasoned cop always understands that each case is different and to approach that case as if he was a rookie, learning everything all over again, and relying on the basics while carefully searching for the truth."

“Reckon that's kinda like my farm,” Billy told Rita. “Each planting season is sure different and no matter how many seasons I've worked through, I approach each new season with a whole lot of caution and a whole bunch of hope.”

Rita saw Brad hit his brakes and ease to a stop at a four-way stop sign. “Billy,” she said, gently applying the brakes, “Valentine DeVivo could have been killed anywhere in Clovedale Falls. My sister and I believe we might know why Joey Stally was killed in the candle shop, but we don't know why Valentine was killed and left behind in your apple orchard.”

“Me, neither,” Billy assured Rita.

“Billy, are you absolutely sure you haven’t hired any new workers?” Rhonda asked. “Anyone who might be...seem out of place. A drifter, maybe?”

“Not a chance,” Billy promised Rhonda. “I know my people like I said, by name and face. Billy Northfield doesn't hire anyone that puts an ugly feeling in his stomach, no sir. I hire honest, hardworking folks who earn every penny I pay them.”

“We figured that,” Rhonda assured Billy. “We have to ask our questions, though. It's all part of the job.”

“I understand,” Billy said as a few drops of rain struck his face.

“We hope you aren't offended, Billy,” Rita asked.

“Nah,” Billy replied, “I ain't a cop but I know that cops have a job to do just the same as a farmer. A dead man showed up on my farm and you girls need to find out why. I'd be mighty dumb to take offense at being asked a few questions. My daddy said a man that refuses to help the law is a law breaker and I don't want to do that.”

Rita eased through the four-way stop and caught up to Brad. “You're a sweet man, Billy,” she said in a sincere voice. “Thank you for cooperating with us.”

“Anytime,” Billy beamed. Being called sweet by a lovely woman sure made his night. “Got any more questions for me? I'd be glad to answer them.”

“Well,” Rhonda pondered, “I'm wondering how Valentine DeVivo arrived in the apple orchards. If I’m not mistaken there is a main gravel road that circles the farm and small dirt lanes that branch off the main road, right?”

“Daddy made it that way,” Billy explained. “Daddy liked math and set the lanes out...kinda like a grid. All the lanes connected back to the gravel road just as pretty as you can imagine.”

“Valentine's car couldn't have driven back to the apple orchards, right?” Rhonda asked.

“No ma’am,” Billy assured Rhonda. “The lanes are for tractor use only, especially in this mud. Any car would’ve gotten mired in an instant.”

Rita studied Rhonda's line of questioning. “Billy, the gravel road has one main entrance, right?”

“That's right,” Billy explained. “The gravel road circles the farm and then ends up right back in front of my house. One way in and one way out. Daddy liked it that way and it sure helps keep out unwanted traffic. Sure is a problem when the festival arrives, though. Cars get backed up a bit...but that's the way it is, I reckon.”

Rhonda leaned her head back on the seat rest and closed her eyes. “Why did you go to Billy's farm, Valentine?” she whispered. “What's the connection? The farm is miles from town...unless...”

“Unless Valentine was intending on doing the killing,” Rita pointed out.

“Either that,” Rhonda said and flung her eyes open, “or he was looking for the money Joey stole from him.”

Rita turned her head toward Rhonda in shock. “I didn't consider that,” she said.

“I didn't either, until just now,” Rhonda replied.

Rita bit down on her lower lip. “Perhaps Valentine went out to Billy's farm searching for stolen money...the killer followed him...and...lights out for Valentine? Is that the idea?” she asked Rhonda.

“I think we're in the general area,” Rhonda answered in an excited voice and half turned around in her seat. “Billy, when you get back to your farm tonight, gather all of your workers.”

“Why, all of my workers will be sound asleep,” Billy objected. “If I roused even one of them, why, I'd be skinned alive.”

“That's a chance you're going to have to take, Billy,” Rhonda said. “I need you to question every last one of your workers and ask them if they have seen anyone on your farm.”

“I tell you,” Billy objected, “ain't nobody been on my farm. If there had been, my workers would have told me. I know my workers by--”

“Face and name,” Rhonda gently interrupted. “We know that, Billy. But look at Jose. He saw a murder take place and didn't immediately tell you. It could be one of your workers saw something...or someone...and is afraid to tell you?”

“I...reckon that's...possible,” Billy caved in. “Fear makes folks mighty tight lipped at times.”

“Yes, fear makes people...folks...mighty tight lipped,” Rhonda agreed, thinking back to a woman who had witnessed a horrible murder but refused to talk because the killer had threatened her life.

“I reckon you want me to call you if one of my workers tells me something?” Billy asked.

“Yes,” Rhonda nodded. “Rita and I would need to be present when you question your workers, but the sight of cops can make a person very nervous. You know your people, Billy. You can make them talk without feeling afraid."

"I reckon I can," Billy agreed and let out a heavy sigh. "Daddy sure wouldn't be happy about this. He taught me to respect the people working for you and treat them like family. That's what I've always done, too. I'm not saying I've never had to chase away a few bad skunks in my day, but most of the people I hire are good, hard-working folk who just want to earn an honest living."

"Billy," Rita said, "listen to me very carefully." Billy sat up, hearing the seriousness in her tone. "Joey Stally could have buried millions of dollars somewhere on your farm. If one of your workers spotted him, well, let's just say there are times when money overrides a person's honor."

"Millions of dollars?" Billy exclaimed. "Ain't no way a person buried that much money on my farm without any of my--" Billy stopped, closed his eyes, and let out a deep moan. "Without one of my workers seeing," he finished. "My goodness..."

Rhonda looked at Billy with caring eyes. "Maybe," she said, "Jose wasn't out taking a walk because he was upset Maria turned him down for supper. Maybe," she offered, "Jose was out looking for hidden treasure?"

"But," Billy begged, "Jose is a good kid. I mean, he did confess to seeing the murder take place, didn't he? He sure did. Ain't no way my kid is a killer...or a thief. Why, I send Jose into town all the time to put money in the bank for me. He ain't never stole a penny from me. We're family."

"Billy," Rita said, "sometimes we have to put our personal feelings aside in order to find the truth." Rita passed a driveway that led to a brightly lit two story home. Town was getting closer. "We're not implying that Jose killed Valentine or stole the hidden money. All we're implying is that it's possible Jose, and maybe more of your workers, know more than you realize."

"And it's your job to find out the truth for us, Billy," Rhonda said. "Brad is taking Jose to the station house to get a statement from him. But Jose has made it very clear that he's not going to do anymore talking tonight."

"The kid is scared," Billy insisted. "That's why he won't talk no more. Just scared."

"Maybe. But that's why you have to talk to him, along with the rest of your workers," Rita explained. "We need help, Billy. Rhonda and I are still strangers in Clovedale Falls and folks aren't going to open up to us. You're a native, someone people love and trust."

"Please," Rhonda begged Billy. "Help out two girls who are new in town."

Billy rubbed his eyes. How could he say no to two beautiful women? "I've always been a sap for a pretty face," he moaned. "In this situation...two pretty faces."

Rhonda smiled at Billy. "I'm sure if your daddy was sitting beside you he would say it's the heart that matters and not a woman's face."

"If my daddy was sitting beside me," Billy told Rhonda, "he would be tanning my backside asking why I hadn't asked one or the other of you girls to marry—uh, someone."

Rita and Rhonda grinned at each other. Billy Northfield was a sweet man who they were both looking forward to calling a friend. Billy was looking forward to making friends with Rita and Rhonda, too. But then his mind began to think about the people working on his farm. Somewhere out in the ~~dark,~~ (delete) rainy, autumn night someone knew the truth, he thought—and that someone might just be living on his farm. His extended family of workers might not be so cozy after all.

7

Rhonda walked into a log cabin kitchen decorated with quaint nineteen-forties style designs that reminded her more of a cottage lost in time on a foggy cliff than a modern cabin. The kitchen smelled of cinnamon and pumpkin spices caressing the air with delicate autumn aromas. "Coffee?" she asked Rita, tossing her purse down onto the round kitchen table covered with a white and red checkered tablecloth.

Rita nodded gratefully. "I'll cook us something to eat."

"Great," Rhonda said. "I'm starving. With all the talking, we didn't get a chance to eat a bite at Erma's."

"I know," Rita complained. She walked to the kitchen table, sat down, took off her high heels, and rubbed her ankles. "My feet are killing me. Tomorrow I'm wearing my running shoes."

Rhonda sat down across from Rita, removed her high heels too, and tossed them next to the wooden back door that a grizzly bear could break through. She sighed. "Let's face it, Rita. We're not the type of women who wear high heels. We decided to wear high heels today only because we wanted to make a good impression on the locals."

"We also didn't think about how we were going to bake—let alone investigate crime—wearing these high heels," Rita pointed out in a pained voice. "From now on let's remain practical and not worry about making an impression."

"Deal," Rhonda agreed. She rubbed her ankles for a minute and then stood up. "I'll make the coffee."

"I'll make us peanut butter and jelly sandwiches and warm up a couple cans of tomato soup." Rita stood up and walked over to a set of wooden cabinets that had been painted with a seaside mural. The mural was so realistic that Rita swore she heard distant seagulls every time she looked at it. "Jose is hiding something," she mused, opening a cabinet and fishing out a fresh jar of peanut butter; creamy, not crunchy.

"I know," Rhonda replied, opening the red and white coffee jar and letting the aroma of delicious coffee grounds take over the kitchen. "Do you think he saw Joey hide the stolen money?"

Rita shut the cabinet and walked over to the vintage Westinghouse refrigerator. "I believe Jose did see Valentine DeVivo get killed...but I keep wondering why he came back to the scene of the crime. I know he's claiming he came back because he was worried about Billy and his family...but something tells me he came back to the apple orchard for another reason."

"To find the stolen money?" Rhonda asked.

"The apple orchard was dark. He didn't even have a flashlight--"

"Flashlights make you an easy target."

"That makes so much sense," Rita replied. "Jose didn't have a flashlight, maybe because he didn't want to be seen. He was wandering around in the dark. If he was looking for people, and knew we were standing close to Valentine's body, he would have presented himself instead of hiding in the shadows until we flushed him out."

"I've been thinking about that, too," Rhonda stated and began filling an old fashioned coffee percolator with water. "The kid was sneaking about."

"Sneaking about searching for stolen money," Rita added.

"Stolen money that Jose clearly doesn't know the location of," Rhonda finished, spooning coffee grounds into the top of the percolator and turning it on. She leaned against the counter next to the sink, thinking.

"Perhaps someone else does know the location," Rita said. "Jose might have heard something from someone he works with."

"Which leaves us hoping Billy will find out something."

“Correct!” Rita replied. “I never would have thought that I’d be asking a Georgia farmer for help solving a murder case.”

“Billy is a sweet man.”

“Of course he is,” Rita agreed. “But Rhonda, let's face it, he's not the type of man who understands a lot of nuances about crime and how criminals think. He's a backwoods farmer. Yes, he's sweet and dear, but he's not like the people we worked with in Atlanta – he’s not exactly a CEO.”

“Isn’t he, though? I mean, he runs his own farm, which is a business. Just because he doesn’t naturally understand criminals doesn’t make him stupid. Billy is better than a fancy suit-and-tie man who claims to understand criminals even though he’s never gotten his hands dirty. Billy helps bring a lot of joy to people. Sure, maybe he's not Einstein, but he's got more decency and common sense in his little finger than most people do in their entire bodies and...and...” Rhonda paused, sighed, and shook her head. “I sound like Dad, don't I?”

“Yes, you do.”

“Billy is a nice guy, that's all I'm pointing out,” Rhonda said and turned to check on the coffee percolator, which was beginning to simmer a little. “I'm confident he'll make Jose talk. I'm also confident he'll get his workers to talk.”

“Jose is a key witness,” Rita told Rhonda. “If he really did see who killed Valentine DeVivo--”

"I believe he did."

"Me, too," Rita agreed. "Jose can close this case for us."

"But the kid is refusing to talk….at least for now. He's scared stiff." Rhonda watched the coffee as it began to percolate up into the crystal knob of the old-fashioned device. "I love this old machine – it truly makes the best coffee." She took a big whiff of the fresh smell of brewing coffee and waited until it was done spitting and bubbling inside before she unplugged it. She focused her mind on the case again. "That young man is trying to find the stolen money because he's scared and wanting to make a run for it with his family. Maybe at first he wanted to find the stolen money for...fun or adventure, or whatever...maybe to have enough money to marry his girlfriend Maria...but now he wants the money to be able to make a clean and safe getaway. Something scared him badly."

"That's my impression, too," Rita nodded. She opened the refrigerator, retrieved a jar of jelly, and walked over to the kitchen counter. "I think Billy knows that, too. I saw the way he was looking at Jose at the station while Brad questioned him. Billy knew Jose was acting strange."

"Brad didn't go too hard on the kid," Rhonda pointed out. "As a matter of fact, Brad was very gentle. Jose wasn't acting strange because he was being questioned by a sheriff, that's for sure."

"You're right. And it was good that Jose was comfortable with him," Rita said. She opened the wooden bread box painted with sunflowers and laid out slices for each of them on plates. “I think Jose had done some thinking on the way to town and decided to clam up.”

“I think--” Rhonda began to speak but stopped when someone knocked on the back door. Rhonda, out of sheer instinct, went for her gun. Rita followed suit. “Cover me,” she whispered. There was no window in the back door, which made them both extra nervous.

Rita ran to the island stove in the middle of the kitchen and hunkered down. “I've got you covered.”

Rhonda nodded and eased over to the back door. “Who is it?” she called out in a stern voice.

“Karina DeVivo,” a woman answered in a scared voice. Although it was hard to hear through the door, she had a thick Italian accent. “Please open, let me in.” Her English was not particularly good.

Rhonda threw a glance at Rita. Rita hesitated and then nodded. “One second,” Rhonda yelled and carefully disengaged the deadbolt on the back door. “Ready?” she whispered to Rita.

“Ready,” Rita whispered back, keeping her gun at the ready.

Rhonda drew in a deep breath and slowly eased the back door open. A lovely forty-year-old woman with the longest black hair Rita or Rhonda had ever seen appeared. “Hands up,” Rhonda ordered, peeking her head out the doorway to check that no one else was lying in wait behind her. It seemed to be just her, however.

Karina DeVivo placed her hands in the air. "I do not have any weapon," she told Rhonda in a shaky voice.

Rhonda glanced down at the long, black trench coat Karina wore and then motioned her to enter the kitchen. "Slowly," she ordered.

Karina stepped into the kitchen, soaked with rain and trembling all over. "Valentino DeVivo, he is dead." It was barely audible through her sobs.

"We know," Rita said, easing up from behind the island stove. "Take off your coat."

"I told you, I am not armed."

"Take off your coat," Rita ordered.

Karina did as asked and removed her black trench coat, revealing a long black dress. "Why do you mafia people wear all black?" Rhonda sighed and motioned for the woman to sit down at the kitchen table. She had a sudden realization. "Wait – are you Valentine's driver?" she asked.

Karina nodded yes as she slowly folded her soaked trench coat over the back of her chair. Slowly she mastered her shaking cries and took a deep breath. "He asked me to accompany him to the United States," she explained, then hesitated, eyes flickering between the twin sisters for a moment. "He said I am going to – how you say – flirt? With man who threaten to kill my brothers."

The sisters were taken aback at this. "We weren't aware Valentine DeVivo even had a daughter," Rita pointed out.

Karina sat up straighter, wiping her tears away. Beneath her tears her face was flawless and dignified, elegant and smoothly composed. "If you were my father, enemies hiding in the shadows everyplace you go, would you go talking about your daughter?" Karina asked. "Or would you keep her safe, hidden, in the old country?"

"I guess you're right," Rita answered. She slowly lowered her gun but remained standing behind the island. "Who killed your father?" she asked. "Did you witness it?"

Rhonda moved over to Rita and lowered her gun so they could both face this unexpected visitor. "Talk to us."

Karina shook her head. "I do not know who killed my father," she replied in a frantic voice.

"Calm down," Rita told the woman before she could start crying again. "Take a deep breath and talk to us."

Karina's tears began streaming down her cheeks again but spoke through them. "My father came here to Georgia because he need to find Joey Stally," she explained and wiped at her tears with her left arm. "This man who was hiding in the FBI Witness Protection Program."

"We know that," Rhonda told Karina.

Karina nodded. "My father had a man on the inside, a source that helped him find Joey," she continued. "The FBI is…difficult. Some kind of internal fighting, all the time, so my father's sources had a very difficult time getting him the information."

"Get to the point," Rita ordered. It was maddening to hear about the corruption behind the scenes, but they could not afford to lose focus on their main goal, not when they were so close.

Karina lowered her eyes, wiped at her tears, and then looked around the quaint kitchen wishing she were back home in Italy. "Very big mouths, always talking my brothers Vinnie and Frank," she snapped in anger. "They brag, always brag. Our father warned them to stay quiet but they never listen." Karina squeezed her hands into two tight fists. "My brothers, very proud men. They want *rispetto,* respect. They want people to fear them. You understand?"

Rita glanced at Rhonda. Rhonda nodded. "I think we understand, yes. Vinnie and Frank ran their mouths about the money Joey stole, didn't they?"

"Yes," Karina nearly hissed. "Told everyone they would find Joey's money when they got out, and be rich men. While they let their tongues run loose, our father was planning how to get them out of the prison. But..." Karina blushed a little, embarrassed.

"But what?" Rita asked.

"My father needed…some money," Karina confessed, clenching her jaw. "The DeVivo Family isn't as wealthy as it once was. Unfair lawyers and corrupt laws take so much from us. My father needed the money Joey stole to get my two idiot brothers out of prison. That is why he put all of his resources into locating Joey."

"What happened when your father finally found Joey?" Rhonda asked.

"Joey was taken to the prison to see my brothers Vinnie and Frank. My father wanted Joey to tell them where he hid the money he stole," Karina explained. "This was the bargain. Joey lives if he give up the money, see? My father is very kind, very wonderful man."

"Did Joey go to the prison?" Rita asked.

Karina nodded yes. "One of my father's men took Joey to see Vinnie and Frank." Karina looked at Rita. "Joey agrees to bargain, and tells my brothers where he hid the money."

"I'm sure Vinnie and Frank believed every word Joey said," Rhonda said and rolled her eyes.

"Of course not," Karina replied. "They would not let him go so easy, they know what kind of man is Joey Stally. They watch him wherever he go, keep watching, until money is found. My brothers, they say to my father, Joey is setting a trap. He has not confessed the truth still. So my father sends another man to...convince Joey." Karina shook her head sadly. "But Joey…he has no faith in my father, in his own boss. What did the DeVivos ever do to him? He ran away. He escapes from his house. I told him it was a mistake to let Joey stay at his own house...my father did not listen. He was too worried that FBI hiding Joey would find out about our little…visits to him for information. That's all. You see? When Joey ran, what choice did my father have? He followed."

"We get it," Rhonda told Karina. "What we don't get is why Joey came to Clovedale Falls. Mind filling us in?"

Karina sighed. "I don't know why Joey came to this place," she confessed with a nonchalant shrug. "All I do know is my brothers Vinnie and Frank were in trouble. My father and I come to follow Joey, and then we hear from my brothers they are in big, big trouble." Karina looked around the kitchen again, distressed. "A threat, a ransom… someone inside the prison, demanding they turn over the stolen money or be killed."

"Warden Miller?" Rita asked.

"Warden Miller, my father thought this too, yes," Karina nodded in surprise. "How did you know? My father said to me, who else could it be?"

Rhonda glanced at Rita again and then focused back on Karina. "Never mind how, we know. Why come to us tonight?" she asked. "Why didn't you just leave town?"

"My father is dead," Karina said, distraught. "You want me to leave my father's body here, and run? No. I drive my father to the farm," Karina explained, "and he died there. I know it. He told me, one hour: if he did not come back, I am to find you, Signorina Rita and Signorina Rhonda Knight."

"Why?" Rita asked.

"For protection," Karina replied, her eyes wide. "My father Valentine hated you for what you did to the DeVivo

Family, but he knows you. You are good people. You would protect me if something happen to him."

"Valentine DeVivo threatened us earlier today," Rhonda told Karina, shaking her head in disgust.

"My father, he is—he was—an old man. Old habits die hard, I think you say."

"I guess," Rita said and focused on a question still rattling around in her mind. "Did your father know if Warden Hank Miller killed Joey Stally? He might have had a hunch, but he didn't know for sure, did he?"

"No," Karina told Rita. "He did not know for sure. This Warden Miller, he is a protected man. My father could not touch him."

"These threats Vinnie and Frank received, surely someone knows who--" Rhonda began to speak.

"Vinnie and Frank were threatened by an inmate acting as messenger and nothing else," Karina told Rhonda and then threw her hands together. "You have to know my father already tried and failed to find Joey's killer. He wanted Joey's money, not his death. What good is Joey to us if he is dead?" Karina took a deep breath and continued. "My uncle believes a *famiglia*, a family, in New Jersey is responsible for killing Joey. When my uncle finds out my father, his brother, has been killed? He will be filled with rage." Karina looked at Rita and Rhonda with desperate eyes. "My uncle is a bad man. Vinnie and Frank cannot tell my uncle the truth. Bad things will happen to them. To many, many people."

Rita looked behind her at the coffee pot. “Looks like we're going to need more than one pot of coffee tonight,” she told Rhonda.

“Tell me about it,” Rhonda said. She looked at Karina, saw a terrified woman who was in mourning and who presented no threat. She sighed. “Miss DeVivo, are you hungry?”

“Very hungry,” Karina confessed. “Please, call me Karina.”

“Peanut butter and jelly sandwiches and tomato soup is for supper,” Rita told Karina and went to fill the coffee percolator once again.

“I would be very, very grateful,” Karina told Rita and Rhonda in a shaky voice.

“I'll be grateful when my headache goes away,” Rhonda said. “This case is causing me to have one major migraine.”

“At least we're getting some answers,” Rita said in a relieved voice.

“Yeah, I suppose we are,” Rhonda agreed and rubbed the sides of her temples. “I just wish I understood why Joey Stally came to Clovedale Falls. Why here? Why us? If he had the money he stole from Valentine DeVivo, why didn't he run to a sunny island in the Pacific, or somewhere else more remote? Why did he come here and possibly bury it in Billy's apple orchard?”

“I don't know,” Rita answered and looked at Karina with careful eyes. The woman was hunched over her coffee mug, clutching her hands around its warmth. “I'm not even sure what to do with her.”

Before Rhonda could reply, the old, tan wall phone hanging beside the refrigerator rang. Brad was calling. He had some important news about Warden Miller.

“Warden Miller isn't at the prison,” Brad told Rhonda when she answered the phone. He sat behind his desk, puffing on his pipe. “Warden Miller hasn't been at the prison in over three months.”

“How did you find this out?” Rhonda asked, keeping a careful eye on Karina.

“I know a man who can get me the answers I need,” Brad explained. “I can't call him too often, but I figured it was time to call in a favor he owed me.” Brad lowered his pipe. “I decided to have him check on Warden Miller for us and I reckon we can handle the rest on our own.”

Rhonda looked at Rita. “Warden Miller hasn't been at the prison in over three months,” she said.

Rita quickly walked a fresh cup of coffee and half sandwich over to Karina and then made her way over to Rhonda. “Any idea where he is?”

“Brad, does your friend know where Mr. Miller is?” Rhonda asked.

"Sure does," Brad told Rhonda. "Be prepared for some bad news."

Rhonda moaned. "This night can't get any worse. Hit me."

"He has been in Europe," Brad said, spilling the bad news into the night. "Apparently, the man has a bad heart, wasn't a candidate for an artificial one and couldn't wait for a transplant here in the states. So he's been in Europe to get his transplant done at a private clinic with slightly...unorthodox methods."

"You mean he bought himself a transplant heart," Rhonda said.

Brad nodded his head. "Yep," he replied. "Hank Miller has been recovering in Spain this whole time."

"Three months is a long time to recover...I guess? I mean, I don't know much about heart transplants," Rhonda told Brad.

"All I know is what my friend told me." Brad took a puff on his pipe.

"This friend of yours...he's pretty reliable?" Rhonda dared to ask.

"My friend could find a penny under the ocean," Brad confirmed. "He's a former CIA agent with more contacts than a German Shepherd has hair."

"Good enough," Rhonda said. She rubbed the bridge of her nose with her left hand and then looked at Karina. "If

Warden Miller isn't our man," she asked Brad, "then we're back to the square one."

"Maybe not," Brad said in a thoughtful voice.

"What do you mean?"

"Well," Brad said locking his eyes on the office window, "maybe Hank Miller did wrong by buying himself a heart...maybe he didn't. I ain't the man's judge. When a man is close to death he can become very desperate. I don't like the fact that money can determine who gets a heart and who doesn't. But that's a conversation for another time," Brad steadied his mind. "This Mr. Miller is a poster boy hired to please the public—a poster boy of a warden who had enough cash to buy himself a heart, which means--"

"He wouldn't need the money Joey Stally stole," Rhonda said.

"That's right," Brad nodded his head. "Surgery isn't cheap, but he also had to pay for accommodations, private nursing, and presumably bribes to move up on the international donor matching registry. He's not worried about cash if he could foot the bill for all of that and take a medical leave from his job."

"I guess not."

Brad puffed on his pipe. "I'm certain Hank Miller, being a sick man, also wouldn't dive into murder. But," he said in a careful voice, "the deputy he left in charge of the prison might."

Rhonda stiffened. "Who are we talking about, Brad?"

"Deputy Warden Brian Young," Brad told Rhonda.

"Did your friend give you the low-down on this...deputy warden?" Rhonda asked in a hopeful voice, keeping Brian's name from Karina, still not sure what she did and didn't know.

"Sure did," Brad confirmed. "Brian Young is a forty-two year old -bum who defended low-lifes in court. He was disbarred for some shady dealings but the state cut him a deal, offered him a job at the prison Vinnie and Frank DeVivo are rotting in." Brad looked down at the notes from his source and wished he were safe at home just then, and sighed. "So this Brian Young became the new Prison Administrative Law Liaison, or PAL Liaison, whatever that is. If you ask me, it's just a made-up title created by some politician. The important thing to know is that this position is just one step below the warden. When the warden is away the PAL Liaison becomes the Deputy Warden."

Rhonda glanced at Rita in a way that told her sister to keep a very careful eye on Karina. Rita nodded, walked over to the kitchen table, and sat down across from Karina and gave the still-tearful woman a reassuring smile. "I'm all ears, Brad."

"Good," Brad said, "because I think I found our killer for us."

"Hit me."

"Brian Young hasn't been at the prison in over two weeks," Brad began. "But, before I put the cart before the horse, let me back up and bit and tell you that Brian Young began his slimy career in New Jersey as a private lawyer working for a mafia family. He relocated to the Atlanta area about five years ago, right before he was disbarred actually, because the family he had been working for put a hit out on him."

"Such is the life of sewer rats," Rhonda stated.

Brad agreed. "Brian Young ran straight into the arms of Vinnie and Frank DeVivo, but not originally under the name Brian Young. He had a new identity as Lou Callone, a small time wise-guy who everyone assumed had just bought and schemed his way through law school."

"This is unbelievable, Brad. I can't believe your guy dug all this up."

"Hey, we go way back. We watch each other's backs," Brad told Rhonda in a caring voice. "Just like, as cops, you and I can always have each other's backs, too."

"You bet we do," Rhonda smiled, feeling proud to have a new friend like Brad in her life. Maybe, at first, she thought, she didn't want to trust Brad, but now she was head over heels for the man's honor and integrity.

Brad smiled, took a puff on his pipe, and continued. "Brian Young, a.k.a. Lou Callone, is a charming enough rat when he wants to be," he said. "The guy ended up dating the governor's daughter. It was during that time that he slowly started breaking away from Vinnie and

Frank DeVivo's protection. I reckon he believed because he had changed his name he was becoming Mr. Big Time and he didn't need to bother with protection from low-lifes like Vinnie and Frank anymore. And to make matters worse, he betrayed Vinnie DeVivo by not defending the guy in court." Brad put down his pipe. "But perhaps you and your sister know something about that, having worked in Atlanta?" Rhonda didn't reply, not wanting to go into it and tip off her sister about who they were talking about now. "Never mind, tell me another time. Anyway, Brian Wilson started working at the prison about the same time as Warden Miller. Not sure if those two are connected in any way, but I do know the Governor himself hired Brian Wilson on at the prison as the new PAL Liaison. My guess he used his influence through the governor's daughter to get such a cushy job – normally you can't get a job like that if you've been disbarred in another state. I guess he must have dug up some stuff that the governor didn't want made public."

"And working in the prison system would give the guy a chance to make some really ugly contacts," Rhonda added.

"Exactly," Brad agreed. "The one thing that Brian Wilson wasn't expecting was to find Vinnie DeVivo at his prison. Vinnie DeVivo was supposed to be locked away in one farther south."

"Yeah, I remember," Rhonda said in a miserable voice. "His lawyer managed to get him transferred because Vinnie decided to give the feds a few tidbits of information. The rat really dodged a bullet, and so did Frank. But those guys know how to play the system."

"Maybe," Brad replied, "but they ran right into the hands of a rat who can have them killed...and wants them dead."

"A rat who knows all about Joey Stally, too."

Brad nodded his head. "That's right," he said and took a sip of his stale police station coffee. "There's more."

"I wouldn't doubt it."

Brad downed some coffee. "Brian Young was dating Vinnie and Frank's sister...some Italian lady named Carrie, or Kari. Also goes by the name Karina."

Rhonda flickered her eyes over at Karina and gave a quick, tense smile. "We know all about that person."

"Good," Brad said, "because this DeVivo woman has a degree in chemistry. According to my contact this woman is a real smart cookie."

"Indeed," Rhonda nodded, panic forming a hard brick in her stomach. She shifted a little so her gun holster was more accessible.

"My gut is telling me Brian Young and this Karina DeVivo woman are working together."

"I wouldn't doubt it at all," Rhonda agreed, watching the woman at the kitchen table take a delicate spoonful of tomato soup.

"Valentine DeVivo couldn't have known who Brian Young was. Maybe the guy knew who Lou Callone was, but not his past as Brian Young," Brad continued.

"I agree," Rhonda said, forgetting Karina for a second and thinking back to her encounter with Valentine DeVivo. "Valentine DeVivo wasn't certain who killed Joey Stally."

"Karina began dating Brian Young, or rather Lou Callone, about a year before Vinnie DeVivo was sent off to prison for murder," Brad pointed out. "During that year, the guy was also dating the governor's daughter."

"Real nice," Rhonda said in a disgusted voice.

"Here's where it gets interesting," Brad continued. "Karina DeVivo found out that Brian Young was double-crossing her and left the country. She returned to Italy and settled back in her childhood home. But," Brad added, "she began making numerous trips back to the states after finding out that Brian Young was the second man in charge at the prison her brother Vinnie was lodged in. According to my contact, Karina and Brian reconciled." Brad leaned back in his desk chair. He felt tired and ready for a good eight hours of shut-eye. "According to my contact, Karina despised her brothers and her old man...maybe the woman found a way to get rid of all of them in one fell swoop? Who knows. But what I do know is that she began searching for Joey Stally."

Rhonda glanced at Karina. The woman was obviously very beautiful—but her beauty was false, covering a deadly black widow. “I was informed that Valentine DeVivo also began looking for Joey at some point.”

Brad read Rhonda's strained tone and leaned forward. “By who?”

“By a person who has really bad taste in...men's clothing,” Rhonda finished lamely, trying to laugh.

“Is Karina DeVivo with you right now?” he whispered.

“You bet,” Rhonda said, chuckling yet keeping her voice steady and official. “Great information, Brad. We're really closing in on the true killer.”

“I'm on my way. Stay safe.”

“Coffee might be cold,” Rhonda replied casually. “Thanks for calling, Brad. See you tomorrow.”

“Be to you in twenty,” Brad said and hung up the phone. He grabbed his gun, checked the clip, and nodded his head. “Sure beats directing traffic.”

Rhonda hung the receiver back on the wall phone, turned, and focused on Karina. “That was the sheriff. He called to tell me about a man named...drum roll please...Brian Young.”

Before Karina could move an inch, Rita had her gun pointed at the woman. “Don't move a muscle,” she ordered Karina.

Rhonda walked over to the kitchen table, grabbed a chair, spun it around, and sat down in front of Karina. “Talk,” she said in a voice that told Karina that the woman meant serious business.

“Right now,” Rita demanded with anger in her eyes. Karina looked up at them with a look of helpless innocence. “My sister and I want the truth, right this second.”

“You can began by telling us why Joey Stally came to Clovedale Falls. The truth, sister. We know your connections to Brian Young. No more lies.”

Realizing that her cover had been blown, Karina decided to play ball. After all, her life was in danger and she did need help; and unfortunately the cops were the only people she could trust, at least until she could put a better plan into place, she thought. Bargaining for time, she took a deep breath. “You know, Joey was never trusting,” she began to speak. Both Rita and Rhonda realized the woman's accent was not quite as thick as she had pretended, and her grammar improved now that her innocent disguise was dropped. “He trusted no one...except you two. You two were the only cops Joey trusted...and right now, you're the only two cops I can trust. My life is in danger and I truly am very frightened.”

“I can see that you're scared,” Rita said in a tough voice, “but unless you talk to us we're going to toss you out to the dog that's trying to hunt you down.”

“That's right,” Rhonda agreed. “My sister and I are retired. We're not obligated to help you or even protect you.”

Rhonda nodded at the back door. “You can talk to us or hit the road.”

Karina focused on the back door. “No...please,” she begged. “I...need your protection.”

“Because Brian Young is trying to kill you?” Rhonda asked.

“Yes,” Karina confessed. “Or Lou, as I first knew him.”

“Okay,” Rhonda nodded. “We'll stop there and go back to Joey. Start talking.”

“I...knew Joey stole millions from my father...so did Brian. But what could we do? Vinnie was sent off to prison and Joey vanished into Witness Protection. The money was as good as gone.”

“So was the romance,” Rhonda told Karina. “It seems that Brian Young was trying to romance the governor's daughter at the same time he was dating you, did you know that?”

“Yes,” Karina said as her face flashed with furious anger. “Brian and I were supposed to get married. Our goal was to force Joey into a partnership, get him to tell us where he was hiding the stolen money. Brian and I were going to take the money and move to Australia, far away from everyone and everything we knew.” Karina gritted her teeth. “When I found out that Brian was dating another girl, no—not a girl, a vicious woman, one who had certain…political goals of her own, I left the country.”

"Why did you come back?" Rita asked.

"I was foolish," Karina confessed. "When I returned to Sicily I wrote Brian a letter....Brian? No, I wrote Lou Callone a letter...the man who I had fallen in love with." Karina shook her head. "The letter was meant to bring me closure. I wrote down my deepest emotions and ended the letter with a sad, but very angry, goodbye."

"Let me guess," Rhonda said, "Mr. Romance wrote you back?"

"Yes," Karina nodded. "My father...he didn't know Lou was Brian Young. As far as Valentine knew, Brian Young was dead."

"A mafia family in New Jersey put a hit out on Brian Young," Rhonda stated.

"Yes," Karina nodded again. "I brought...Lou to Vinnie and Frank and asked them to help him. Vinnie and Frank agreed. They bought Lou a fake birth certificate, social security card. and driver's license."

"How nice of them," Rita told Karina. She grit her teeth; the woman did not seem to express the tiniest shred of guilt about all this illegal activity.

"Vinnie and Frank blackmailed Lou to be their attorney in return for helping him with his new identity," Karina explained. "Lou was never the one to be pushed around. He's the type of man who understands the game. It wasn't long before he started making friends with some very powerful people."

"And after a while he ditched Vinnie and Frank, right?" Rhonda asked.

"And me," Karina told Rhonda, feeling her anger race across the cheeks on her face. "Only...I was foolish enough to go back to him."

"Why?" Rita asked.

"Lou is in charge of the prison Vinnie and Frank are at--"

"Second in charge," Rhonda corrected Karina. "Warden Hank Miller is first in command."

"Warden Miller needed a new heart, which made Lou the head man," Karina snapped before she could control her temper.

"Ah, I see," Rhonda said, "did your degree in chemistry finally pay off?"

Karina quickly lowered her eyes. She was in serious trouble and unless she wanted to live...she had no choice but to talk to the cops. "I injected a poison into Hank Miller's coffee that harmed his heart," she confessed in a miserable voice.

Rita and Rhonda looked at each other. Now, they thought, the case was finally catching steam and moving down the tracks. "Keep talking," Rhonda ordered.

Karina raised her eyes and looked at the back door. Somewhere out in the night, Brian Young was lurking, waiting to kill her...and anyone else who dared to stand in his way.

8

"When Valentine tracked down Joey Stally I saw an opportunity," Karina said and slowly took a sip of coffee.

"By that time Brian...uh, Lou..." Rhonda said and quickly rolled her eyes. "For now let's just call the rat Brian. Brian was threatening to kill your brothers, Vinnie, and Frank DeVivo."

"Yes," Karina agreed and continued. "I was telling the truth before – my father didn't have the wealth he once had and couldn't afford the ransom Brian demanded in order to spare Vinnie and Frank. As I mentioned before, finding Joey was the only option."

"And you were responsible for bringing that option to light, weren't you?" Rita asked.

"Yes," Karina confessed and took another sip of coffee, clutching her delicate fingers around the mug to catch its fading warmth. "I ordered Brian to start threatening Vinnie and Frank in order to make Valentine pay a ransom. My plan was to..." Karina looked Rhonda and Rita in their eyes. "I wanted Vinnie and Frank dead...call me a monster, but I despised my brothers for the way they treated Lou. And I despised my father for the way he treated everyone...for the people he hurt and killed. But most of all, I despised Lou for...breaking my heart. They all had to die."

"I bet," Rhonda said, reading the finality and glittering serenity in Karina's eyes.

"I had Valentine where I wanted him," Karina said in an angry voice. "I was allowing his anger to build, like a storm, before I confessed to him who Brian Young truly was. I was going to wait until Brian killed Vinnie and Frank and then reveal the truth." Karina drew in a deep breath. "I knew once Vinnie and Frank were dead, my father would risk returning back to the United States and kill Brian with his own hands."

"Trapping Valentine DeVivo for murder, which would lock him in prison for life," Rita pointed out.

"A prison he would die in," Karina spat. "My father would rather be tortured than wind up in prison. His freedom is...or was...very precious to him."

Rhonda leaned forward in her chair. "Let's focus back on Joey," she said.

"Joey presented the perfect chance for me to lure Brian away from the prison," Karina explained. "Valentine surely couldn't walk into a heavily guarded prison and kill him. No, I needed a plan and Joey was the perfect door to open." Karina looked down at her mostly empty coffee mug and then continued. "I went to Joey one night," she said in a low voice. "Joey...was always a little in love with me, from a distance. I knew I could use that. I...warned him that my father was going to kill him...and then I told him who Brian Young truly was. I begged Joey to tell me where he had hidden the stolen money, saying I wanted to run away with him." Karina raised her eyes the way a furious wolf would after losing its prey: hungry, determined, dead set on blood. "Joey recorded every word I spoke and threatened to tell Valentine I was betraying him...unless I married him."

"Not the brightest fella," Rhonda rolled her eyes.

"Tell me about it," Rita agreed in a disgusted voice.

"I panicked," Karina confessed. "Joey had betrayed me--"

"What you mean is Joey outsmarted you," Rita pointed out. "You thought you were being a very smart cookie but fell victim to a paranoid low-life." She resisted pointing out the illegality in Karina's scheme, too, though the whole matter was exasperating. "Are we supposed to feel sorry for you?"

Karina glared at Rhonda with furious eyes. "Fine. Hate me." She shook with anger but stayed in her chair though she looked like she would rather jump up, grab Rhonda by her hair, and sling her across the kitchen. Instead she simply said, "I ran to Brian and begged him to help me...not telling him the complete truth, of course. I made

Brian believe Joey was obsessed and threatening to kill me unless I agreed to marry him."

"I'm sure you didn't let Brian off the hook that easy, though," Rita told Karina. "A woman like you wouldn't let a crisis go to waste without working it to her advantage."

Karina looked at Rita and started to understand a horrible truth: cops weren't as stupid as she once believed. In fact, Karina admitted to herself, cops—at least ones like Rita and Rhonda—were far smarter than she would ever be. It embarrassed her that they saw through her so easily so she barreled ahead with her story. "Brian had to die...Joey had to die...Vinnie, Frank...Valentine, my father...everyone had to die," she exclaimed in a desperate voice. "My life was in danger...it was either me or them. The rules of the game had changed."

"That's…one perspective on the situation," Rhonda told Karina and stood up. She exchanged an incredulous look with her sister. "Keep spilling the beans."

Karina ran her hands through her hair. "I told Brian that I would arrange to meet Joey at a remote location," she said. "I would...bring a poison to stop a heart instantly...and Brian would inject Joey with it. Brian agreed, but...but..."

"But what?" Rita asked.

"Brian knew Joey visited the prison and spoke with Vinnie and Frank. He honestly believed Vinnie and Frank knew where Joey was hiding the stolen money." Karina shook her head. "Brian refused to kill them, insisting Vinnie and Frank be kept alive until they told him where the money was. He threw them in the hole and ordered me to start romancing Joey."

"One way or another Brian Young was going to become the owner of the stolen money, huh?" Rhonda asked.

"Brian was in trouble," Karina explained, her eyes looking more desperate as she realized how thin of an excuse it truly was. "I didn't know it at the time but he had acquired a great deal of gambling debt. His own life was on the line. He didn't tell me this until I went to him about Joey. I sensed that Brian was on edge about something...I just didn't know what. Brian was desperate for money and then he--"

"He stopped being Mr. Nice Guy and threatened to kill you unless you did what he ordered," Rita finished for Karina.

"Yes."

Rhonda joined in. "Joey ran before you could romance him, didn't he?"

"Yes," Karina confirmed, her eyes downcast. "Joey called me and told me he had located the both of you and that he was going to contact you and ask for protection. He ordered me to meet him in this town and marry him before he contacted you, though. I agreed. I came here because I had no choice. Because I needed to stay alive."

"You mean because you saw a way to kill Joey, Brian, and Valentine in one sweep and then go back for Vinnie and Frank later," Rita told Karina.

"Yes...yes...yes," Karina screamed in frustrated rage, unable to control herself.

"Cool down," Rhonda ordered. "Your actions are nothing new to us, sister. We've seen it all. Murder comes in all different forms. You're not the first person to plan a murder, get in a mess, and squirm trying to get free and start taking desperate actions. You're not to blame for the abuse, but there are still crimes to answer for, here. Murders have been committed."

"That's right," Rita told Karina. "At first, we thought maybe the killer was trying to start a mafia war...and maybe you are? After all, Lou Callone did work for a mafia family in New Jersey. It wouldn't be hard for you to turn two families against one another, now would it?"

"I--" Karina began to speak.

Rita held up her hand. "You're nothing special, Karina DeVivo. You may look into a mirror and believe you see a beautiful, charming woman who can outwit any opponent who stands in your path, but deep down you're nothing but a common street thug with murder in her veins. You just happen to dress nicer."

Rita's words slapped Karina across the face. "I'm not a common street thug," she hissed. "I was born into a prestigious family that happens to have been torn by very violent events and—"

"Save your sob story for the courts," Rhonda told Karina, "and let's get back to Joey."

“You are obviously very smart, figure the rest of the story out for yourself,” Karina scowled.

“We already have,” Rita assured Karina. “You agreed to meet Joey in Clovedale Falls and marry him. You conned your father into bringing you here as a driver and a part of his own plan, when you in fact intended to betray him. You also brought Brian along. Only you're a very smart woman, Karina, and you have that degree in chemistry.” Rita locked eyes with Karina. “Brian Young believed the poison he injected into Joey was some form of a truth serum, didn't he?”

Karina’s eyes grew wide with shock. “How did you...I mean...it's impossible--”

“We're cops,” Rhonda told Karina in a proud voice. “It's our job to discover the truth no matter how many lies get piled on top of it.”

“That's right,” Rita said feeling pride swell in her heart. “Cops—good cops—understand how to do their jobs. Now,” she said, “let's move on.”

“I...” Karina stuttered and then caved in. “I was supposed to meet Joey in front of the bakery you two bought. Joey believed I wouldn't dare try to harm him in front of the bakery...it was a way to see...to test me, to make sure I wasn't hiding any cards up my sleeve.”

“A long-range rifle could have ended Joey's life,” Rhonda pointed out. “Standing in front of our bakery wasn't foolproof.”

“Joey was smart in some ways and dumb in other ways,” Karina explained. “He always had a childlike mind.”

“I suppose that could be true,” Rita admitted. “Joey Stally never appeared to be the type of guy who understood the streets very well. Sure, he knew how to watch his back, but he also let Vinnie and Frank discover that he was stealing from the bets.”

Rhonda looked at the back door. It was getting time for Brad to arrive. “How did Joey end up in the candle shop?”

“Brian and I arrived in town earlier than Joey,” Karina explained. “We crawled up onto the roof of a building that faces your bakery.” Karina looked down at her hands, wondering how two such brilliant hands had turned sour, and then looked up. “We spotted Joey arrive right before the sun rose. Joey was nervously smoking a cigarette and began pacing around. He tried the door knob on the front door of your bakery and when he found it locked he tried the front door to the candle shop.”

“Let me guess,” Rhonda sighed, “the door was unlocked.”

“Yes,” Karina answered. “Joey hurried inside and closed the door.

“Maybe he thought he found a way to watch you without being seen?” Rita asked.

“What Joey was thinking didn't matter,” Karina replied and focused on her empty cup.“Brian told me to stay on the roof while he snatched a syringe full of the poison I created out of my purse, and...went off to kill Joey.”

Karina looked up at Rhonda. "Brian had a gun...he simply circled around, came up on the front door to the candle shop unseen, hurried inside with his gun drawn, and took Joey by surprise."

"Brian must not have been happy that the truth serum turned out to be poison," Rhonda ventured.

Karina shook her head no. "He wasn't," he replied. "But you must understand, I was the one who was supposed to talk with Joey, not Brian. Brian was only supposed to watch. My assignment was to lead Joey to a hotel room--"

"A hotel room that Valentine was aware of," Rita interrupted. "After all, you arranged for Valentine to come to Clovedale Falls, didn't you?"

"I was supposed to meet Valentine at nine sharp at a small air strip twenty miles south of town," Karina nodded. "Valentine was flying in on a private plane. I had the car ready...and yes, I had Brian in place."

"Only Brian broke the rules," Rita pointed out.

"Brian didn't trust me to talk with Joey," Karina confessed. "I...panicked and ran. I drove the car I had prepared for Valentine out of town and raced to the air strip...leaving Brian high and dry."

Rita looked at Rhonda. Rhonda bit down on her lower lip. "If you left Brian Young high and dry, how did he kill Valentine? Valentine was poisoned."

Karina drew in a scared, nervous breath. “Brian called my cell phone and demanded I meet with him. He threatened to kill Vinnie and Frank and pin their murders on me if I didn't. I knew Brian was telling the truth, but I also knew if I met him...he would kill me. So I devised a meeting between him and my father, insisting to Valentine that I tracked down the killer. My father...oh, he was such a fool. He believed every word I told him...because I was his darling princess, his prize daughter.” Karina made a disgusted face. “My father kept me hidden away like a crown jewel for years...for my own protection, he always told me. I was told what to eat, what to wear, where to go, who to talk to...and when I became a grown woman and wanted to stretch my own wings, he...he...”

“What?” Rita asked.

“Simply wouldn't stop,” Karina answered in a sour voice. “Even though I grew to see him for who he really was. How could I ever accept love from a monster? I saw the horrors he committed...the people he hurt. My father was a monster who deserved to die. So yes, I arranged his death. I called Brian and told him where Valentine was going to be.”

“How did you choose the location?” Rita asked.

“Valentine cherished his vineyards,” Karina explained. “The closest thing I could find was the apple orchards.” Karina tapped her wrist. “While Valentine was speaking with you two earlier this morning I drove around and scouted out the location. I drove into the country, found a road leading to some farm, parked, and scouted around on foot, unseen and unheard."

"That's a lie," Rhonda told Karina. "You went to find the money Joey had hidden."

"We know the money Joey stole from the bets is hidden somewhere on the farm you went to," Rita snapped at Karina. "Quit playing around. Valentine wasn't a stupid man and wouldn't have arranged to meet Brian Young without having the stolen money in hand. And Brian Young wouldn't have ventured into the orchard without solid evidence that you had the money."

"Brian didn't kill Joey, you did," Rhonda informed Karina. "You saw Joey sneak into the candle shop and you killed him, but not before Joey confessed to you where he was hiding the stolen money."

Karina, realizing she had been trapped in her own lies, felt her hands become sweaty with panic. Trying to blame the murder of two men on Brian Young wasn't working.

"Woman," Rita growled, "stop with the half-truths, do you hear me?"

"I...yes, I hear you," Karina shakily responded.

"Brian Young isn't even in Clovedale Falls, is he?" Rhonda asked.

"He is now," Karina confessed. "But...no, he wasn't...not this morning. I...Brian did threaten to kill Vinnie and Frank and blame their murders on me. That's the truth. He sent me to Clovedale Falls to get the truth out of Joey...with a false truth serum I claimed I created. That's the truth. I decided to kill Joey and Valentine myself. That's the truth."

"Leaving Brian Young, Vinnie, and Frank," Rhonda pointed out.

"I had to lure Brian to Clovedale Falls," Karina explained. "Joey did confess to me where he had the stolen money hidden. I...killed him with a kiss and a poison needle. I left his body in the open...my intention was to cause a war between two families." Karina tried to settle her mind, though the memory disturbed her. "Afterward I drove out to the farm Joey told me about, found the location of the stolen money, dug up the money, took a photo, sent the photo to Brian's phone, and then reburied the money."

Rita looked at Rhonda. "She had evidence that the money had been located and power to lure two men to their deaths," she said and walked her eyes back to Karina. "Both Valentine and Brian were now trapped in your web."

"A woman will always outsmart a man," Karina replied in a dark tone that gave Rita and Rhonda both the creeps. "It was time to end the game once and for all. Daddy's little girl was about to bring out her claws. After all," Karina said, "Joey had helped me regain control."

"Maybe Joey did help you," Rita told Karina. "But look how you repaid him."

"But you're not sitting in our kitchen because you want to be here. Brian Young obviously has you running scared for some reason," Rhonda finished and looked at the back door. "The only question is...where could a wet rat like Brian Young be hiding in Clovedale Falls?"

Rhonda was about to ask Karina another line of questions when the telephone rang. She hurried and answered the call. "Hello?"

"This is Billy," came a worried voice down the line.

"Billy?"

"Yeah, you told me to call, so I reckon now's the time," Billy said and began pacing around a large parlor that never left the nineteen-twenties. "I sent Jose to fetch me his folks," he explained. "When Jose didn't bring his folks I went out to their house on the north side of the farm."

"And no Jose?" Rhonda asked.

"No Jose," Billy said in a voice stricken with worry and fear. "If anything happens to that kid I swear I'll blame myself."

"Okay, Billy, just sit tight. Rita and I are on our way."

"Wasn't sure which one of you I was even speaking to," Billy admitted. "You ladies are going to have to start wearing name tags or something."

"I guess we will," Rhonda told Billy with a small smile. "Give us about twenty minutes. The sheriff is on his way-

-" Before Rhonda could finish her sentence Brad knocked on the back door. "I think the sheriff is here now, Billy."

"Just hurry," Billy pleaded. He snatched up a piece of peppermint in an antique crystal candy dish and popped it into his mouth. "Get here before I eat every piece of candy in this blasted house...my poor blasted nerves...that blasted kid. We should all be in bed at this hour of the night. Why, if my daddy was alive he'd be fussing up a storm. And let me tell you, Chester isn't happy about being kept up this late, either. Why, he's twitching both of his ears right and left."

"We'll hurry," Rhonda promised and hung up the phone. "Brad?" she yelled.

"Yeah, it's me," Brad yelled through the back door.

Karina tensed and began to stand up. "No, you don't," Rita said. She pointed her gun at Karina and motioned for her to sit down as Rhonda opened the back door.

"Rain is still coming down pretty hard," Brad said as he stepped into the kitchen and began shaking rain off his poncho. "This her?" He asked looking down at Karina with careful eyes.

"Say hello to Karina DeVivo," Rita told Brad, lowering her gun.

Brad stopped shaking rainwater off his poncho, pushed the back door closed with his left foot, and said "put cuffs on her."

"Hand me a pair," Rhonda told Brad.

Brad reached under his poncho, retrieved, and tossed to Rhonda. She took them and walked over to Karina, and slapped them down onto her wrists.

"Is this really necessary?" Karina complained.

"Yes, it is," Rhonda said and quickly turned her attention to Brad. "Billy just called. He said Jose is missing."

Rita shot up to her feet. "Let's get out to his farm," she replied in an urgent voice, completely caught up in the case. The thought of the bakery, the Pumpkin Festival—and even Clovedale Falls itself—was far from her mind. All Rita cared about was bringing justice to the guilty.

The case, she thought, focusing her attention on Brad, might seem confusing to a rookie, but to her, the technical complications presented themselves in the form of human thought. She understood the mindset of criminals, how they thought, and how they panicked and struggled to reorganize when their original plans became unraveled.

Karina DeVivo had believed she had the perfect plan to murder six people, when in truth, she had forgotten to take into account the harsh forces of reality and the raw unpredictability of human beings that lurked on levels that would never be understood. Karina DeVivo was nothing but a common killer who was going to face justice, along with Brian Young, Rita promised herself, feeling like a cop in action again; the feeling swept through her as natural as breathing. "Brad, take Karina down to the station and throw her behind bars and then meet us at Billy's."

Brad didn't take offense at Rita's order. Instead he respected Rita's commitment to duty and admired her passion for justice. “I shouldn't be too long,” he said and nodded at Karina. “On your feet.”

Karina slowly stood up. So much for a hot meal, she thought, looking longingly at the plate and soup bowl on the table. The day—and her lies—had caught up to her. Only gray skies and cold prison food awaited her...unless she somehow cut a deal with the cops. After all, she thought, it wasn’t impossible to manipulate the justice system. Even though she had failed to play Rita and Rhonda to her advantage in order to force them to protect her, she could still easily claim that she was a victim to the feds and offer them information on certain mafia families in return for her freedom. But, Karina warned herself, the feds were far away and Brian Young was running free, intent on ending her life. “Sheriff,” she said, “a man wants to kill me. If you lock me up, he might reach me. Please,” she begged, “keep me in your custody.”

Rita glanced over at Rhonda. Rhonda bit down on her lip. “Maybe it would be better to keep her within arms’ reach?” Rhonda said.

Rita considered her sister's suggestion and then agreed. “I think so, too. There is no telling what Brian Young is doing or where he is. We need to--” Rita was interrupted by the telephone. “That could be Billy again. I'll answer it.” Rita ran over to the phone and answered the call. “Billy?”

“I want Karina DeVivo and the money within one hour, or two very scared people are going to die,” hissed a voice that could only be Brian Young. The sound sent chills down Rita's spine.

“Help us!” Rita heard Jose’s voice cry out in the background of the phone call.

“Shut up!” Brian yelled.

“Please don't hurt us!” Rita heard a young girl beg.

“Jose and Maria,” Rita whispered and motioned for Rhonda to hurry over to the phone. “Okay, Brian, take it easy. We're listening,” she said in a calm voice and held the phone away from her ear enough in order for Rhonda to hear the conversation. “We have Karina. But we don't have the money.”

“Don't lie to me!” Brian hollered into the phone. “I know Karina has the money. She betrayed me. She tricked me into going into that orchard and then took a photo of me standing over Valentine DeVivo's body.” Brian hit a wooden wall he was standing close to. “Karina ordered me to release Vinnie and Frank DeVivo and threatened to send the photo to all of my enemies if I didn't...that little liar!” Brian hit the wall again, bruising his fist. “I'm as good as dead! My only chance is to get that photo from her. I almost had it, too...but that woman managed to escape from me.”

Rita looked at Karina. “Escape?” she asked.

"Yeah, escape!" Brian gritted out. "I was stupid enough to let her use the bathroom, okay? I had her hands tied together but...I was stupid, okay?" Brian growled under his breath. "I won't make the same mistake twice. Bring me Karina and the money or I'm going to kill the two brats I have with me."

"And where are you?" Rita asked.

"Oh no, I'm not that stupid, cop," Brian hissed. "I'm tired of being played. I let Karina play me long enough. I should have known she didn't love me...I should have known she wanted revenge after I went behind her back and sweet-talked the governor's daughter. Love...how stupid was I?"

"Enough with the drama," Rita snapped.

"You said it," Brian growled. "You have one hour."

"One hour and no location, genius," Rita plowed into Brian. "I'm a very practical woman who can't read minds. If you don't tell me what location to go to--"

"Okay, okay," Brian said. He threw his eyes at Jose. "Bring Karina and the money back to the apple orchard, same spot you found Valentine DeVivo's body at," he told Rita. "Leave them there and take a hike. I'll be around. If I see you playing any tricks then I'll slip away and kill these two brats."

Rita looked at Rhonda. "We could cut you a deal," she told Brian. "Karina has confessed to killing Joey Stally and Valentine DeVivo. All you're doing is making the situation worse for yourself."

“How?” Brian yelled. “I'm probably already dead. As far as I know Karina has already texted her uncle the photo of me standing over Valentine DeVivo's body.” Brian ran his left hand through his sweaty black hair. “I doubt I'll get the photo from her, but I have to try. What I really want is--”

“The money,” Rita told Brian. “You need to escape a lot more people other than the mafia families who might be coming for you. It seems you have a lot of gambling debt?”

“Karina has been running her mouth real good, I see,” Brian said sarcastically.

Rita and Rhonda could both clearly hear that Brian was on the verge of breaking. The man wasn't thinking clearly, was panicked and desperate to stay alive—a bad mix. When a man was trapped in Brian’s state of mind he became extremely dangerous, uncontrollable, and very unpredictable. “Brian, let us help you. You haven't harmed anyone yet--”

“Don't,” Brian yelled. “Don't play your cop games with me, lady. I know your kind. You don't care about me.” Brian looked over at the pretty Hispanic girl cradled up next to Jose. The girl trembled with terror and cowered in his gaze but he didn't care. It was Brian Young against the world; Lou Callone was dead. “Bring me Karina and the money in one hour or else.”

Rita bit down on her lip and quickly studied the new development. She decided to make Brian believe he was in control; an old trick cops used. “Okay, Brian, just don't hurt Jose and Maria. We'll do what you say...just don't hurt Jose and Maria, please."

"One hour...the apple orchards," Brian snapped and slammed the phone down.

Rhonda ran over to Brad. "Brian has Jose and Maria. He's demanding we bring Karina and the money Joey Stally stole back to the apple orchards in one hour," she explained.

"No, you can't do that," Karina exclaimed.

"Shut up," Rhonda ordered Karina. "Brad, that scumbag is on the verge of a mental breakdown. There's no telling what he might do. You have to go find Jose and Maria. Those two kids have to be somewhere in Clovedale Falls."

Brad rested his hand on his gun. "Clovedale Falls isn't very big but the county is massive," he pointed out. "I don't have the manpower to search every house. Not in an hour."

"Not houses," Rhonda pointed out, "rental cabins."

"Rental cabins?" Brad asked. "How do you know that?"

"Brian's voice," Rhonda explained. "I can tell he's standing in a large, open room." Rhonda looked back at Rita. "Brian isn't calling from a hotel room or his vehicle," she continued. "And I'm sure he's not going to risk breaking into somebody's home. It has to be a rental cabin, the kind with those open living rooms and high cathedral ceilings."

Brad didn't waste any more time questioning Rhonda. The woman had sense to her that he trusted. "Okay," he said,

"I'll get my guys, call up some reserves, and start searching every rental cabin in the county," he assured Rhonda.

"What about me?" Karina begged.

"You're staying with us," Rhonda informed Karina.

"That's right," Rita said and checked her gun. "Looks like we're going to catch pneumonia after all, Rhonda."

Rhonda glanced down at her bare feet. "Not in high heels," she stated. "I'll run upstairs and get our running shoes."

"Please do," Rita said in relief, "because I couldn't walk another step in my high heels."

Rhonda nodded and dashed out of the kitchen. "I better get going," Brad told Rita.

"Please wait until Rhonda comes back," Rita told Brad, not wanting to be alone with Karina. It wasn't that she was afraid of the woman physically. It was the fact that Karina DeVivo gave her the creeps; every killer Rita had ever encountered gave her the creeps. Why? Because killers were like black widow spiders...soulless and without heart. "I can pour you a quick cup of coffee?"

"That'll be fine," Brad said and ordered Karina to sit back down.

Rita began making her way over to the coffee pot and then without warning made a sudden detour back to the phone and called Billy. "Billy, this is Rita. Is Chester still awake?" she asked. Brad gave Rita a strange look, scratched the back of his neck, and waited.

"Awake and cranky as ever," Billy told Rita. "Why?" He walked over to a green armchair older than time itself and plopped down. Chester, lying on his usual rug, twitched his right ear at Billy. "I saw that!" Billy barked at Chester. "It ain't my fault this night is sour."

Rita rolled her eyes. A man and his dog, she thought. "Billy, I need you to listen very carefully," she said in an urgent voice. "We know who has Jose and Maria."

"Why didn't you say so?" Billy asked and jumped to his feet. "Tell me who the varmint is and I'll go get my rifle and hunt him down."

"That's very brave of you, Billy, but at the moment we have to remain practical and not let our emotions cause us to make mistakes," Rita explained. "At the moment I need Chester's help. Chester is a bloodhound, right?"

"Why, he sure is," Billy exclaimed. "Best dog in all the county. Chester can hunt down a flea in a swamp."

"I was hoping you were going to tell me that," Rita told Billy and looked at Brad with a small grin. "I'm going to need Chester to smell a very dangerous woman for me."

"A woman?" Billy cried out. "For Pete's sake, why?"

"Because the low-life who has Jose and Maria was with this woman earlier today," Rita explained. "She might have, uh, gotten her scent on him."

"Oh," Billy said and then grinned. "I got you and I'm completely on board. Let's just hope Chester will be, too...you cranky ol' dog."

Brad folded his arms. Rita sure was one smart cookie. "Now this is police work," he whispered and looked down at Karina. Karina was staring at Rita with hate in her eyes and death ~~in~~ (on) her mind. Rita didn't care. Karina was learning a hard truth: cops weren't as stupid as she once thought. Cops—real cops—had something criminals didn't: common sense.

9

Chester stared at Karina with curious eyes and a stiff tail. Whoever the strange woman was standing in his parlor sure wasn't a friendly person. The woman smelled of badness, which made Chester want to bite her. Chester didn't like people who smelled of badness. The bad smell on people always went along with someone getting hurt and Chester hated that. "Easy, boy," Billy said, spotting Chester's scruff raise up. "Don't go getting all upset over a sourpuss."

Karina stepped back toward Rita. "Don't let that mangy dog bite me," she snapped in a fearful voice.

"Chester wouldn't hurt a soul," Billy told Karina. "He's just letting you know that you smell of no-good is all." Billy sniffed the air. "I can smell the no-good on you, too. Shame, too, because you're a mighty pretty woman. My daddy always did say that it don't matter what a woman's face looks like if her heart don't match. Reckon that's true with you."

Chester let out a low growl. “Easy, boy,” Rhonda whispered and gently patted Chester on his head. Chester looked up at Rhonda, smelled the goodness on her and sensed the good in her heart, and stopped growling. “Billy,” Rhonda said, “Brian Young is desperate. From the few minutes he spoke to Rita on the phone I was able to conclude that he's not a very smart person, either.”

“He's a con man,” Rita told Billy. “He's the type that can charm a piece of candy away from a child but can't stand up under real pressure.” Rita turned to Karina. “Isn't that right?”

Karina frowned. “Brian never did have...problem-solving skills,” she admitted. “Brian is the type of person who...thinks on his feet, focuses on the moment...a bit naive about tomorrow, perhaps.”

“You sure picked a winner to love,” Billy said and shook his head. “I'll never understand why some women don't have enough sense to settle down with a decent fella. World is full of decent fellas but some women don't have enough sense to see that.”

Rita and Rhonda both looked at Billy at the same time. Billy Northfield, they thought, was a decent fella. But before they could say so, Karina continued to talk. “Brian had charm,” she told Billy defiantly. “He was daring, funny, interesting and a little dangerous...at least when his life wasn’t in danger. I...honestly believed Brian was a brave knight...not realizing that, underneath, he was a coward and a...con man.”

“Reckon you can't be blamed for bein’ played,” Billy told Karina in a kind voice. “Ain't my place to judge, either. The good Lord will do the judging and, whew, that's a day this old boy fears.” Billy rubbed the back of his neck. “I know Jesus loves me, but ain't a person alive that ain't sinned, and like my daddy always said...we're all gonna answer for what we've done.”

Billy's words struck Karina deep in her heart. “Can we...get on with the matter at hand?” she asked in a shaky voice.

“You bet,” Billy said. He reached down, grabbed Chester by his collar, and cautiously walked the dog over to Karina. “Get a few whiffs,” he told Chester, “and see what you think.”

Karina tensed up as Chester locked eyes with her. “Brian...grabbed me,” she explained. “I wasn't wearing my trench coat at the time. We...struggled with each other...I managed to escape. His scent should be on my dress...”

Billy sniffed at Karina. “Yeah, I can smell the faint scent of cologne...not much, but some.” Chester raised his nose and sniffed at Karina’s dress. The dress smelled of something new and bad, some sweet-smelling flower, and coffee, and something that reminded him of the water his master splashed on his face after taking a shower and brushing his teeth; the fancy-smelling water. It was a big scent, and it was bossy and bad and all over.

“Got the scent, boy?” Billy asked. Chester flapped his left ear. “He's got it.”

"Good," Rita said. "All we have to do now is ride out into the rain. I'm sure Brian is around by now."

Rhonda checked her gun. "Okay, Billy," she said, "it's time to let Chester loose. I just hope I can keep up with him." Rhonda smiled at Chester. "Don't get too far ahead of me, boy."

"You ladies sure about this?" Billy asked in an uncertain voice. "It's sure raining cats and dogs, and it's darker than black tar outside. I'm not so sure it's smart to be fiddling around--"

"Billy," Rhonda spoke in a caring voice, "We understand the dangers."

Rita walked up to Billy. "Brian Young isn't a threat," she explained. "Brian Young is a coward that will run at the first sign of a threat."

Billy looked into Rita's eyes. The woman sure was rubbing off on him. "You sure?" he asked. "I hate to leave you out there unprotected. I can get my rifle and--"

"We're sure," Rita promised. "Now, put a muzzle on Chester to keep him from barking. We need him to track Brian Young for us, not scare him off."

Billy shook his head. "Chester sure ain't gonna like having a muzzle put on him. That dog is going to be grumpy at me for weeks to come. He needs his mouth to sniff."

Rhonda smiled. "We'll repay Chester's good deed with a month's worth of hamburgers."

Billy looked at Chester. Chester flapped his right ear. “Ain't gonna be good enough,” he said, pulled a muzzle from his front pocket, and sighed. “Okay, boy, time to work,” he said and carefully attached the muzzle over Chester's mouth. Chester plopped down on his backside and gave Billy a doleful look. “I know...I know...but the ladies need you to be tracking that skunky smell without all the baying and howling that goes along with it. They need you to be real quiet and let's face it...you ain't quiet when you get after a skunky smell.” Chester flapped both of his ears. “Now don't start,” Billy fussed.

“Has it really come down to this?” Karina asked, watching this hillbilly of a man fuss with his sloppy looking dog. At least, she reminded herself, there was still a good chance to make a deal with the feds and secure her freedom. But still, she thought, standing in an old parlor, handcuffed, and watching a farmer talk to his dog certainly was humiliating for a woman of her intelligence.

Rita and Rhonda read the expression on Karina’s face and shook their heads. “What is it?” Karina asked.

“You're standing there still thinking you're better than everyone in this room,” Rita told Karina. “I feel very sorry for you.”

“You can feel sorry for me after I'm free,” Karina snapped before she could control her tongue. “I'll cut a deal with the feds and be back in Italy before you can blink an eye. I'm not going to lose this game.”

“The tragedy,” Rhonda spoke, “is that you're probably right. The feds will cut a deal with you because you're a small fish. You're not a threat to them but you probably have information that they want. So yes, the feds will most likely cut a deal and you'll receive a warning and a light slap on the wrist and then be sent home to Italy. But before any of that happens, you're going to learn a valuable lesson tonight.”

Karina was tired of the lectures. Her plan to manipulate Rita and Rhonda had failed. The two women were obviously smarter than she was and had clearly seen through her plan. How? Karina didn't know. She had thrown half-truths mixed in with real emotions, fear and tears enough to deceive any man...only Rita and Rhonda weren't men, and they weren’t ordinary women, either. “Save your lectures,” she snapped.

Rhonda walked up to Karina and locked eyes with her. “I've always had a good sense of humor,” she said in a voice that made Karina back down. “I enjoy jokes, pulling pranks, and even laughing in the worst of situations. I believe in smiling, laughing, and keeping a positive attitude. But you, sister, turn my stomach sour and take all the fun out of living. So you listen and listen very carefully.” Rhonda pointed her right finger at Karina. “My sister is going to accompany you back to the orchard and you're going to do everything she tells you, is that clear?” Karina began to speak but Rhonda told her to shut up. “My sister is a deadly shot and she won't hesitate to shoot. Billy will be close by and he's a dead aim with his rifle. Am I making myself clear?”

"I...understand," Karina told Rhonda, backing down from her sour attitude. "Please, protect my life. That's all I ask of you."

"Your job is to be a decoy," Rhonda explained. "I'm sure Brian Young isn't standing out in the open waiting to be nabbed. He's hiding someplace, but you better believe he's watching." Rhonda turned to Chester. "It's time, boy."

Rita put a hand on her sister's shoulder. "I had to lose the coin toss, didn't I?" she said in a miserable voice.

Rhonda looked down at her running shoes. "I'll be okay," she told Rita and forced a confident smile to her face. "I have Chester."

Rita pulled Rhonda into her arms. "Don't hesitate to shoot," she begged.

"The same goes for you," Rhonda whispered and hugged her sister back.

Rita felt a tear touch her eye. "I can't lose you."

"And I can't lose you," Rhonda replied. "Who else would fuss at me for putting a smiley face sticker on an old cash register, huh?"

Rita wiped at her tear. "Don't start," she tried to smile but failed. "Rhonda...shoot first if you have to."

"I will," Rhonda promised and focused on Chester. "Let's go, boy," she said and raced out of the parlor before Rita could stop her.

"Okay," Rita said drawing in a deep breath, "it's time to do our job. Billy, go get the tractor ready."

Billy nodded his head and left the parlor. "What about me?" Karina asked.

Rita grabbed Karina's handcuffed wrists. "You're coming with me," she said and pulled Karina out into the rain, up onto the wagon, and then pushed her down on a damp bale of hay. "When we reach our location you better do as I say," she ordered Karina.

Karina listened to the heavy rain falling and then heard Billy crank up the tractor engine. Fear gripped her stomach. What if Brian was hiding in the rain with a rifle? What if Brian had no intention of speaking with her? What if Brian just wanted a clean shot at her? "No," Karina whispered, "Brian is desperate...and he's dug his own grave. These women cops are too smart for him."

"You bet we are," Rita told Karina as Billy got the tractor moving.

"There they go, boy," Rhonda told Chester standing behind a tree. "It's time for you and me to get moving." Rhonda quickly bent down, placed her hands around Chester's ear and said: "Please go find the bad guy, boy." Chester, even though he was now drenched in rain and very muddy, looked into Rhonda's eyes, saw the good, and then wagged his tail. "Good boy," Rhonda beamed. "Let's go."

Chester felt Rhonda let go of his leash. He wagged his tail again, sniffed the air, and started running toward the apple orchards, following the bad smell. Rhonda pulled out her gun and followed, running through mud puddles, over rocks, through wet grass, past a copse of trees, around work buildings, and finally arrived at a lane leading into the apple orchard. "Love my running shoes," she said breathing hard, "hate...being in my forties."

Chester, sensing that the woman needed to rest—smelling her sweaty exhaustion—stopped, sniffed the wet air, sniffed the ground, thought for a minute, and then pointed north and wagged his tail. "You...smell him, boy?" Rhonda asked, putting her hands down onto her knees. Chester wagged his tail again. "Okay...let's go." Rhonda leaned up, raised her face into the rain, calmed her mind, and then patted Chester on the head. "Let's move." Chester wagged his tail, licked Rhonda's left hand, and took off running.

Rhonda drew in a deep breath and got her legs moving. She ran after him into a row of apple trees and began struggling over fallen apples and uneven ground as one tree branch after another grabbed at her. "Keep moving," she whispered, spotting Chester in the distance. Chester paused, sniffed the air, and then turned right and dashed into another lane. Rhonda ran into the lane as quickly as her feet would take her, fearful she was losing Chester. But to her relief, Chester was waiting for her. When Chester spotted Rhonda he hurried deeper into the apple orchard. "He's hot on the scent," Rhonda continued running. "Remind me to boycott apples after this."

Chester ran up to an apple tree, looked over his shoulder, spotted Rhonda, and started wagging his tail. Rhonda zoomed up to Chester and bent down. "What is it, boy?"

she whispered. Chester locked his eyes forward. Rhonda walked her eyes through the rain and began searching the dark apple orchard. At first all she saw were shadowy silhouettes. “I don't see anyone,” she whispered, straining her eyes. “I don't--” Before Rhonda could finish her sentence she spotted a shadow run out from behind a tree and hurry behind another tree. As the shadow vanished, the sound of Billy's tractor reached Rhonda's ears.

“Chester, I love you,” Rhonda whispered and kissed Chester on his wet nose. Chester looked up at Rhonda and wagged his tail. “Stay here, okay? Stay.” Rhonda checked her gun and then eased back into the darkness and circled around behind the shadow.

As Rhonda moved into position, Brian Young hunched down behind an apple tree and watched Billy's tractor appear. “That's right,” he hissed and quickly examined the rifle in his wet hands. “Time to die, cops.”

Billy pulled his tractor to a stop and looked around. Something in his gut told him that a mean snake was hiding out here. But what could he do? Rita and Rhonda seemed sure of themselves and, well—like his daddy always said: friendship without trust was a pie without filling. “Okay,” Billy said, opening the tractor cab door, “let's do this.”

What Billy didn't know as he stepped down from his tractor was that Brian Young had a rifle aimed straight at his back.

Brian peered through the powerful rifle scope and watched Billy walking toward the back of his tractor. He waited. “Let's see what we have,” he whispered. Billy went to the wagon, attached the wooden walk plank, and helped Rita down. Seconds later Karina appeared. “Bingo,” Brian grinned and focused his rifle back on Billy. “Time to die,” he said and began to squeeze the trigger on the rifle.

“I don't think so,” Rhonda yelled.

“Huh?” Brian jerked and spun around on his knee. He was met by a dead tree limb swinging into his face with intense force. The tree limb smacked him straight in the head. It broke in two but not before sending Brian into dreamland.

“Ouch...splinters...splinters...” Rhonda cried out in pain and began pulling shards of shattered wood from her hands. Despite the rain, the limb she had found was quite dry.

Rita, sensing that her sister was close by, searched the rain. “Rhonda is near,” she told Billy, making the mistake of turning her back to Karina. Billy, assuming that Karina was no longer a threat, turned away from her and studied the darkness. Karina realized this was her chance. She quickly looked down at the gun Rita held, examined her handcuffed hands, and then decided to act; never realizing that she was falling into the same trap any desperate criminal fell into. With one swift motion she threw her right leg out at Rita, hitting her hard in her left leg. Rita let out a painful scream and began to topple down onto the muddy ground. As she did, Karina snatched the gun out of Rita’s hand and stepped back away from Billy.

"Don't move!" Karina yelled.

Rita scrambled for her footing in a mud puddle. "Don't make this worse than it has to be," she told Karina as the heavy rain soaked her face. "You won't get far."

Billy stared at Karina with angry eyes. "You had no right to hurt this lady," he roared and bravely stepped in front of Rita.

"Get back," Karina hissed.

"You ain't worrying me none," Billy snapped, "so go on and get out of here. The law will track you down soon enough. I know this farm like the back of my hand. You won't get more than a mile before you'll be begging for me to get you out of the woods."

"I'll leave after you help me dig the money back up," Karina growled at Billy. "All I want is the money and a vehicle."

"Oh, go dig up that money yourself," Billy fussed. "I ain't gonna lift another finger for you, do you hear me?"

Rita took Billy's hand. "Help me stand up, Billy."

Billy, with loving care, helped Rita stand up, Rita gently rubbed her left leg and then wiped mud off her dress. "Run, Karina," she said, "because that's what you're going to be doing for the rest of your miserable life."

"Shut up!" Karina yelled. "Who do you think you are, anyway? I'm Karina DeVivo. The DeVivo Family always wins," she announced in a voice that came out far too shaky for her liking.

Rita stared at Karina and watched the rain fall down the woman's doomed face. "Do you?" she asked and motioned around with her eyes. "Where is Brian?"

Karina jerked her head from side to side and studied the darkness. Brian Young was nowhere to be seen. "I suppose your sister captured him," she said and slowly took a step back. "Both of you...get back in the wagon...now!"

"Nah," Billy said, "I'd rather you shoot me first, cause I ain't gonna expose my friend and die a coward."

Karina was used to lowlifes who bowed down at the first sign of danger—men who pretended to walk tough but were nothing but cowards deep down inside of their hearts; men who wore fancy suits and carried guns meant to disguise the yellow-bellied dogs that they truly were. Billy Northfield wasn't one of those men. And for some reason that struck Karina deep in her soul. Why? She had no idea. All Karina did know was that Billy Northfield wasn't a coward—he was a real man. "Get into the wagon," she yelled.

"Nah," Billy said again spotting Rhonda easing up behind Karina and grinned.

"This isn't funny!" Karina hollered. "Do what I say or--"

"You're going to shoot them?" Rhonda asked.

Karina nearly jumped out of her skin. She spun around and saw Rhonda pointing a gun directly at her. “Don't shoot!” Karina cried and threw down Rita's gun. “Please don't shoot me!”

Rhonda rolled her eyes. “Sister,” she said, “you play the part of stupid real well.”

Rita let out a sigh of relief, ran over to Rhonda, and hugged her. “Where is Brian Young?”

“Out cold and handcuffed to a tree,” Rhonda explained as she hugged Rita back. “I saw her kick your leg. Are you okay?”

“A little embarrassed. For a woman who prides herself on being very practical I made a very stupid error.”

“Won't be the last time,” Rhonda teased.

“Thanks a lot,” Rita joked and then smiled. “We solved this case in one day, Rhonda. Do you know what that means?”

“The bakery,” Rhonda laughed. “Do you really want to stand here in the rain and chat about it? But you’re right, we still have time to get our bakery in order before the Pumpkin Festival starts.”

“Exactly,” Rita beamed. “And who cares about the rain? Now, about the antique shops. Since Erma has offered to give us her old items I think we can use the money we put aside for--”

“For our savings, right?” Rhonda groaned.

“That would be the practical solution,” Rita answered, feeling an argument about to begin. “Rhonda, we have financial obligations to meet and we must be very practical in our spending.”

Rhonda sighed. “Billy, help me out,” she begged.

Billy shrugged his shoulders. “My daddy always said that a man who decides to get in between two fussing women is a man who is hungry for a beating. I ain't hungry for no beating.”

“I guess not,” a voice said.

“Huh?” Billy asked and swung around. He spotted Brad walking up with a very wet and scared Jose and Maria. “Why, I'll be.”

Jose bowed his head in shame. “I saw that woman digging up the money, Billy...I...wanted to...I mean...”

“Jose wanted the money for us,” Maria cried. She stepped out from under the umbrella Brad was holding over her head. “Jose and I want to get married and start a family, Billy. Please don't be mad at him.”

Billy frowned. “You did a mighty dumb thing, Jose.”

“I know,” Jose apologized in a sorrowful voice. He lifted his head and pointed at Karina. “I was out here trimming the apple trees and saw that woman dig up a black briefcase full of money. I thought she was going to take the money but all she did was take some photos with her phone and put the money back in the ground. I...waited until she left and took the money...and buried it. When it got dark I went to get it...and that's when I saw that woman...kill that man. I ran away," Jose continued. "All I could think about was the money...and Maria. Later I decided to go back for the money...and that's when I saw the lawmen standing near the body." Jose broke down into tears. "When we came home from town tonight I went to Maria, told her the truth...and together, we decided to go for the money."

"That terrible man who kidnapped us was hiding in the orchard," Maria cried. "We're sorry for all the trouble we caused, Billy. Please don't send us away."

"Send you away?" Billy asked in a shocked voice. "Now," he said and put his arms around Jose and Maria, "folks do silly things all the time. Why, my daddy said if you sent a hunting dog away the first time he didn't run down a fox, why, you'd be sending away your meal ticket." Billy pulled Jose and Maria close. "You come from some real fine folks...folks Billy Northfield is honored to call his friends. I ain't gonna send you away nowhere but home to those folks. You learned a lesson in the end, and you're safe now, that's what's most important. Now get going because the sun is going to rise mighty early on all of us and we have a full day's work ahead of us."

Jose stared at Maria in shock and looked up at Billy. "You mean, you're not mad?"

"Aw," Billy said, "you kids are just peeking your heads out of the ground. You ain't full grown beanstalks yet. You still got a lot of learning to do and I intend to help you along the way. Now scoot on home."

"But not before you tell us where the stolen money is," Rita said in a quick voice.

"Oh yeah," Billy said, "I reckon you better fess up, Jose."

Jose eagerly agreed and walked everyone to an unremarkable spot under an apple tree and pointed down at the ground. "The money is under this tree. I marked the tree with a line of green spray paint." Jose looked at Karina. "I moved it, you see. You would have dug up an empty hole...sorry."

"Don't be sorry," Billy told Jose, "her kind ain't worth being sorry over." And with those words, Billy walked Jose and Maria away.

Brad looked at Rita and Rhonda. "Found the kids in a rental cabin down by Peppermint Lake. You were right."

"We were lucky," Rita pointed out. "Blessedly lucky."

"We sure were," Rhonda said and then yawned. "My, this night has caught up to me," she told Brad and handed Karina over to him. "She's all yours now. My sister and I are going home to get some sleep. We have to be at our bakery bright and early...with working shoes on and not high heels."

"If I can ever dry out first," Rita sighed and looked up at the rain. "All I want is a peanut butter and jelly sandwich, a bowl of tomato soup, a hot bath, and a soft, warm bed."

Brad smiled. "You ladies did real good," he said in a proud voice.

"Don't smile yet," Rhonda told Brad and pointed north. "Brian Young is handcuffed to an apple tree. You're not going to get home any time soon."

"I have my guys standing by," Brad assured Rhonda. "Tonight they're learning that being a cop isn't a nine to five job." Brad focused on Karina. "People like you make for long hours."

"They sure do," Rhonda agreed and yawned again. "Come on, Brad, and I'll show you where Brian Young is and--" before Rhonda could finish her sentence, Chester appeared. "Why, hello there Chester." Chester wagged his tail and walked up to Rhonda. Rhonda bent down, removed the muzzle from over Chester's mouth, and kissed his wet nose. "You were wonderful." Chester licked Rhonda on her nose.

"Now cut that out, Chester," Billy said, reappearing in the rain. "I can't leave you alone for a second before you start turning into Romeo?"

Rhonda laughed. "Leave this handsome guy alone, Billy. He's my hero."

"Yeah, yeah," Billy complained with a smile and pointed back toward his farmhouse. "Chester, you and me got to get some sleep. Come on." Chester flapped his right ear. "Now don't start with me!" Billy huffed. "It's been a mighty long day and I still got to get up with the rooster." Chester flapped his right ear again. "Fine, stay out here in the rain. See if I care. Night all," Billy said and wandered back toward his tractor. Chester finally let out a whine and chased after Billy, galumphing up into the cab of the tractor after his master.

"True love," Rita laughed and walked away with Rhonda and Brad.

The next morning, Rita and Rhonda trudged into their bakery half-asleep, dressed in gray jogging outfits, and carrying a cup of coffee apiece. "What a night," Rhonda sighed.

"Tell me about it," Rita agreed, leaning against the front counter. "At least the case wasn't that difficult to solve."

"It would have been if Karina DeVivo hadn't decided to play her games," Rhonda pointed out and then let out a wide yawn. "If Karina hadn't tried to manipulate us into helping her we would still be up a river without a paddle. There were a lot of twists and turns in the case that we didn't catch."

"No one is perfect," Rita yawned.

"That's not a very practical response," Rhonda teased.

"Don't start on me," Rita complained. "My hair is a mess, my makeup is all smudged and my coffee is getting cold."

Rhonda smiled. "I know," she said and hugged Rita.

“What was that for?” Rita asked.

Rhonda motioned around the bakery. “Well, sister of mine,” she said, “here we are, two retired cops standing in a bakery that needs a heap of work and living in a town with some mighty interesting characters in it. I would say we're doing just fine for ourselves.”

Rita gazed around the bakery and then looked out the front window and spotted the fresh autumn leaves falling. The rain had passed, leaving behind a crisp, cool morning filled with the scent of pumpkins, apples, and the promise of a beautiful season. “We're going to be okay, aren't we?” she asked.

Rhonda squeezed her sister’s shoulder with a loving hand. “You bet we are. We're going to get our bakery in shape and be ready for the Pumpkin Festival. And on top of that,” she added in a warm voice, “we're going to be happy. We're going to be very, very happy in Clovedale Falls because we're surrounded by some really good people. People who make life worth living.”

Rita stared into Rhonda's eyes, felt a wonderful hope touch her heart, and smiled. “I believe we are going to be happy,” she agreed and hugged Rhonda. “Now, let's get to work. One of us has to go get the moving truck while the other starts trying to move the old appliances outside.”

“I'll go get the moving truck,” Rhonda said in a quick voice and started to race toward the front door.

Rita reached out and grabbed Rhonda by the back of her sweatshirt. “I'm the one with the sore leg,” she announced, "and any practical person knows that a woman with a sore leg doesn't need to try and move heavy appliances. I'll go get the moving truck and you start moving the appliances outside."

Rhonda moaned to herself. "Being practical stinks."

"Not all the time," Rita giggled sweetly, grabbed her purse and coffee, and left the bakery. Rhonda watched her sister leave then slowly walked into the kitchen with a huge smile on her face. So what if she was stuck with the hard job? Life was good. The bad guys were behind bars. And the Pumpkin Festival was going to be open for business with two sisters proudly selling their baked goods and joining their fellow townspeople in the celebrations.

"As Billy would say," Rhonda said, focusing her attention on scrubbing the old stove, "life without problems would only make a wheel go flat, but life with some hard work makes the wheel go round and round...or something like that," Rhonda laughed and got to work in the light-filled kitchen.

As she did, a nervous teenage girl, far away on the West Coast, boarded a bus and began a long journey straight for Clovedale Falls, not knowing that a deadly killer was following her every move.

ABOUT WENDY

Wendy Meadows is a USA Today bestselling author whose stories showcase witty women sleuths. To date, she has published dozens of books, which include her popular Sweetfern Harbor series, Sweet Peach Bakery series, and Alaska Cozy series, to name a few. She lives in the "Granite State" with her husband, two sons, two mini pig and a lovable Labradoodle.

If you enjoyed this book, please take a few minutes to leave a review. Authors truly appreciate this, and it helps other readers decide if the book might be for them. Thank you!

Get in touch with Wendy

www.wendymeadows.com

CPSIA information can be obtained
at www.ICGtesting.com
Printed in the USA
LVHW011623011121
702139LV00011B/1324